Born and raised just outside Toronto, Ontario, **Amy Ruttan** fled the big city to settle down with the country boy of her dreams. After the birth of her second child Amy was lucky enough to realise her lifelong dream of becoming a romance author. When she's not furiously typing away at her computer she's mum to three wonderful children, who use her as a personal taxi and chef.

A DATE WITH
DR MOUSTAKAS

AMY RUTTAN

MILLS & BOON

Published in Great Britain 2018
by Mills & Boon, an imprint of HarperCollins*Publishers*
1 London Bridge Street, London, SE1 9GF

© 2018 Amy Ruttan

ISBN: 978-0-263-07647-9

ROM

This book is pro   led FSC™ paper
to ensure responsible forest management.
For more information visit www.harpercollins.co.uk/green.

Printed and bound in Great Britain
by CPI Group (UK) Ltd, Croydon, CR0 4YY

This book is dedicated to my Medical Romance girls, Tina, Annie and Amalie.

You three are an amazing inspiration to me.

PROLOGUE

Nashville, Tennessee

HE HATED HIMSELF for what he was about to do.

Don't do it, then.

Dr. Christos Moustakas stared down at the contract on his desk—the one he'd just signed for a job that would take him away from Nashville and away from Naomi.

He was angry at himself for getting involved with her. When he'd first seen her—when they'd been placed on the same surgical resident rotation last year—he'd known that he shouldn't even pursue her. Naomi was the type of woman who wanted far more than he could give.

He never wanted to get married. He never wanted to settle down. He had told her that in the beginning, but now…despite his warnings…he knew that she wanted more from him and he just couldn't give it to her.

Why not?

Chris cursed under his breath and walked away from the contract. He looked about his apartment, which was full of memories of him and Naomi together. She was in his blood…she was all he ever thought about.

And he couldn't have that.

Work was more important.

He had to end it now.

There was a knock at the door and his heart skipped a beat. His jaw clenched and his stomach churned, because he knew that he was going to break her heart.

But it was for the best.

He didn't want to marry her and lock her into an unhappy marriage—just like what had happened to his parents.

He *never* wanted that.

Naomi beamed at him when he opened the door, and leaned in to kiss him on the cheek as she came into his apartment.

"There you are! What's up? You've been a bit distant recently..." She trailed off as she saw the boxes in the apartment. "Oh."

Chris shut the door. "Yeah, sorry I haven't been returning your calls, but something came up."

"I see that," she said quietly, and then turned around. "Where are you going?"

"New York City. I've been offered a fellowship with Dr. Heffernan in neurosurgery, and then I'll take over his practice when he retires later next year. I'll be the head of neurosurgery."

"Wow, that's amazing. Congratulations... When do you leave?"

"Tonight."

Her face fell and he knew that it had hit her. "You were going to leave without telling me?"

"No, that's why I asked you over."

You're a monster. You're just awful.

"I thought..." She shook her head. "I don't know *what* I thought."

"Tell me." He could take it, and he deserved her wrath. He deserved it all.

For one brief moment he wished he was a different person—but he wasn't, and he couldn't see how to change. He knew what it was like to grow up with an absent mother who hated and loathed your very existence and a father who couldn't look at you because you were a disappointment.

Families were complicated and messy.

He wanted none of it.

"I thought we would talk about our offers together," she said. "I mean, I turned down Mayo because I thought you wanted to be with me."

Her eyes were full of tears and he fought the urge to take her in his arms and comfort her.

"Why didn't you take the job at Mayo?" he asked.

"I should've, apparently."

"Yes, you should've, Naomi. This is your career. It's important."

"I didn't want to leave you. I wanted to give us a chance!"

He closed his eyes, pain washing over him, but he hardened his heart. He shouldn't have gotten involved with her to begin with. He should've walked away after that first stolen kiss that had electrified his world.

Naomi Hudson was dangerous, and he'd known that all along—but he'd still pursued her.

"You should've taken the job, Naomi. There *is* no long-term future for us. I told you this at the start."

A tear slipped down her cheek. "I remember, but I thought—"

"You thought what?" he interrupted. "That I would change my mind? My goal has always been to make it to head of neurosurgery. You *knew* this."

"And *you* knew, deep down, that I wanted more from our relationship and yet you kept me dangling. You kept pursuing me. You didn't let me go either!" she shouted.

"I'm letting you go now," he said stonily, his heart breaking because he didn't want to let her go, but it was for the best.

"I thought I meant more to you," she said, her voice shaking.

"Look, we both knew this had to end sometime."

"I *didn't* know that. Or I guess I just didn't want to believe it."

"Well, then, that's *your* problem."

And he hated himself for saying those words, but they needed to be said. He had to put an end to it. She'd given up a job for him, but he'd never asked her to do that. She had to move on from him.

The sting of her slap on his cheek didn't catch him off guard. He was expecting it.

"Enjoy New York, you bastard! I hope to God I never see you again!"

She pushed past him, and he didn't turn around as the door opened and then slammed shut behind her.

Instead he sighed, felt a tear almost slipping from his eye. He wandered to the window, watching her get into her car and drive away.

When had he become such a coldhearted monster like his father?

He was selfish, greedy. He'd wanted her so badly, and for a year it had been bliss. Then she'd started to creep her way in through his carefully constructed walls. She'd started to plan for a future that he had never wanted.

It was time to let her go—even if his heart really didn't want to.

She would find someone better than him. Someone who deserved her. He was not the man for her.

He didn't deserve her, but he would never forget her.

There would never be a woman like her for him again—he'd make sure of it—and he was also sure that he would never love another woman the way he'd loved her.

There would only ever be one Dr. Naomi Hudson in his life, and he'd just thrown her away. She'd be happier without him, and he'd be miserable without her, but it served him right.

He picked up the contract for the job in Manhattan again. This was what his life was all about—saving lives. In some ways, at least, if he excelled at his job, it might make up for the hurt he'd caused her.

At least he could do something good with his time... even though his life and his heart were beyond saving and always would be.

CHAPTER ONE

Three years later, Mythelios, Greek Islands

ANOTHER SLEEPLESS NIGHT.

The heat wasn't helping. Even though he'd been back in Greece since the middle of July—two months after the earthquake—Chris still wasn't quite used to the temperature. His body was firmly set to Manhattan mode and Manhattan temperatures. It also didn't help that the island of Mythelios was still recovering from that earthquake.

His late grandmother's home didn't have air-conditioning either. And, since the island still remained in repair mode, renovations that weren't crucial to the infrastructure and safety of the citizens had been put on hold.

Air-conditioning would have to wait.

He yawned as he opened the doors to the small terrace of his grandmother's beautiful villa. He leaned over the balcony, watching the sun rise over the Aegean Sea.

It had been a long time since he'd watched the sun rise bright and beautiful over the turquoise sea of his youth. It had been years since he'd picked olives in his grandmother's garden or swum in the sea. The garden was overgrown now, but up on the top level of the house he had an unobstructed view of the horizon.

His grandmother's home was the oldest and the highest of the old homes that had been built into the cliffs of Mythelios. It had thankfully fared pretty well during the earthquake, only suffering slight damage, while newer homes had suffered and crumbled.

It was funny how it had managed to stay intact through the powerful quake.

It was funny how nothing really seemed to have changed here since he was a young man.

He'd been in America for so long, pursuing women and his career, that he'd forgotten to stop and smell the roses—or in this case the orange blossoms that wafted up from his late grandmother's garden.

His life for the last three years in New York City had been endless parties, women and work. Work had been his priority. He'd let nothing get in the way of becoming the top neurosurgeon on the eastern seaboard.

Well, that wasn't quite accurate. One thing *had* gotten in the way—and that was the reason for his sleepless nights and why he'd returned to Greece.

An ill-fated one-night stand in a long string of the one-night stands he'd had in order to get over losing the woman he truly loved had led to him having a baby dropped off on his doorstep. Well, not so much on his doorstep. He'd paid a lot of money to the mother so he could keep his son.

Baby Evangelos was his world now, and even though Chris could afford a nanny, and had one for his infant son, she was entitled to take a night off—as she had last night. He was on feeding and diapering duty whenever that happened.

Chris scrubbed a hand over his face.

Why had he let his life go completely sideways like this?

When had it gotten to be so hard?

Right—he knew exactly when *that* had happened: when he'd walked away from Naomi and put his career before love. That was when it had all gone to heck. He'd left behind the only woman who had ever broken down the careful walls he'd created to keep people out. She'd started to come even before his work, and that had annoyed him.

He'd sworn he would never settle down—not after watching his parents' disastrous marriage crash and burn.

So he'd left her. Frozen her out and left her behind in Nashville while he pursued his high-flying career in New York City. And even worse, she'd loved him and he'd held her back. He hadn't been able to give her what she'd wanted, and yet she'd turned down an excellent job for him. That guilt still ate away at him.

He hadn't been able to forget about her. So he'd tried moving on by bedding a series of different women. And that was how he'd ended up with Evangelos.

And there was no question that he loved his son. He loved being a father—something he'd never thought that he'd ever want—but this was not how he had pictured his return to his home village.

"Nice abs!"

Chris frowned and then looked down to see Ares walking through the square in the tiny village. His long curls were hidden under a baseball cap—one that Chris had sent him when he first went to America.

Ares had been one of his best friends since he was a child. He was one of the four founders of the Mythelios Free Clinic and he worked in emergency medicine. All his friends were back on Mythelios now, since the earthquake, when one of their number—Theo—had put out a call for their help.

Ares had boyish good looks, and the silly hat that Chris had sent him as a joke looked so out of place on him, but it made Chris smile nonetheless. He was glad to be back with Theo, Deakin and Ares, even though they were working in the clinic and he wasn't.

Of course none of *them* had a baby yet.

"Put a shirt on!" Ares teased again, laughing.

"Where are you off to?" Chris called down, ignoring the teasing.

"The clinic. Actually, I was going to come see you. There's a case I'd like your opinion on."

"I'm not here to practice medicine. I came back just to lend a hand and deal with my grandmother's death."

"Come on," Ares begged. "I need your expert opinion. Besides, it's high time you got your hands dirty at the clinic *you* helped found."

Ares had a point—and he did miss working. He missed neurosurgery.

Chris nodded. "Okay. I'll come by when Lisa comes back."

Ares raised his eyebrows. "Who's Lisa?"

"Evan's nanny."

"Ah, and here I thought the infamous Greek Valentino of Manhattan was up to his old tricks."

Chris snorted. "And since when do I have time for that?"

"Well, you must've had *some* time," Ares teased. "You're the only one with a kid."

Not for long, since Cailey Nikolaides was four and

a half months pregnant now. Cailey was a nurse at the clinic, and Theo's wife.

"Look, either come into the house or get to work. You're going to wake the neighbors with your incessant shouting in the streets!" Chris called.

Ares winked. "See you in a couple hours."

Chris watched him jog away through the narrow alleyways of the old part of the island, where other villas like his grandmother's clung to the side of a cliff by the sea. The homes were brightly colored and connected by narrow cobblestone streets that eventually wound their way down to a large square dominated by a church, and then there was a small path to the docks and to the clinic.

The bell at the church rang out the time, waking up this sleepy island that was only an hour's ride by ferry to Athens, a city much more modern in comparison to the simple way of life that still dominated Mythelios.

He yawned, stretched and looked down.

Dammit.

He wasn't wearing anything at all. Good thing the balcony was solid, and not an open terrace like they had in the larger cities, because he'd fallen asleep naked.

He had to get some clothes on fast, before Lisa came back.

He didn't want to give her the wrong idea.

That had been his problem his whole adult life—he seemed to give all the women he met the wrong idea. Even Naomi had gotten the wrong idea about him in the end.

"I thought I meant more to you," she'd said, her voice shaking.

"Look, we both knew this had to end sometime."

"I didn't know that. Or I guess I just didn't want to believe it."

"Well, then, that's your *problem."*

His stomach clenched as he recalled some of the last words he'd said to her. It cut him to the quick how badly he'd hurt her, but he'd told her from the start he didn't want anything serious.

And it still killed him that she'd given up that job at Mayo for him. He'd held her back and that would haunt him forever, but there was no way he was ever going to settle down with one woman for the rest of his life.

He'd watched his parents.

Once marriage came into play, everything went south. His mother had left, and no matter what Chris had done, he'd never been able to please his father.

He shuddered. He was *never* going to get married.

Chris reluctantly walked away from the balcony and headed back inside. He pulled on a robe and checked on his son, who was sleeping peacefully in his crib. The only fan in the entire house was in the nursery, but even that just pushed around the hot air.

You never wanted to be a father either, a little voice reminded him.

And yet here was Evangelos.

He smiled at his son, so like him, sleeping peacefully. He was sucking the chubby fist in his mouth in his sleep. His dark curls were plastered to his face from the heat.

This island was his world now. He'd do right by Evangelos. His son would never want for anything and would never feel like a stranger to his father—a toy that would be played with only when it suited his parents. Chris was going to make sure his son had everything he could possibly need.

Except he won't have a mother.

Chris shook that thought from his mind.

Evan didn't need a mother. *He'd* made do without a mother's love, and he'd give his son enough love for both parents.

He closed the door to the nursery and headed back to his room, where he had a quick shower and then pulled out the scrubs and lab coat that Theo had given him when he'd returned to Mythelios a few weeks ago.

"What are these for?" Chris had asked as he'd stared down at the scrubs that Theo had handed him.

"They're scrubs."

"I know that," Chris had said, "but what are they for?"

"Look, I know that your *yia-yia* just died, but when you feel the need to come back and work, we could really use you at the clinic."

"Thanks. I'll think about it. If you need me for an emergency, I'll be there, Theo, but I can't commit right now."

"I know," Theo had said gently. "But these are yours for when you need them."

It might not be the glitzy Manhattan hospital where he'd been working, but at least he'd still be working. He would still be doing what he loved and he would be giving something other than money back to his home. His time and his skills.

Ever since he'd headed to America, he'd had a financial hand in the clinic that Theo ran, using his trust fund from Mopaxeni Shipping to help fund it year after year the same way his friends did, but he'd never done more than that.

It was time to do more now, and he'd still be able to devote enough time to Evangelos, and to fixing up his grandmother's home, and to raising his son in a place that was safe and quiet. A place where he'd always been happy when he was young.

Chris was mad at himself for staying away for so long, but he'd thought life would be better in America.

He'd slipped on his clothes and was tying his shoes when the front door opened.

Lisa blushed when she saw him. "Sorry, Dr. Moustakas. I meant to come back sooner, but my cousin from America arrived in Greece a month ago, and she was visiting my family last night in Athens."

"It's okay, Lisa. I gave you the day and the night off. You deserve a break."

Lisa ducked her head and brushed back one of the errant strands of her dark brown hair behind her ear. If he'd been a younger man, and not a father, he would have flirted with her. Only, he wasn't that playboy anymore, and Lisa was from a respectable Athens family. A family that would be expecting a proposal of marriage from any man she became involved with.

"I'm headed down to the clinic. I can be reached there," Chris said as he opened the door, and then he turned back. "How long is your cousin in Athens for?"

"For a while. She's working there," Lisa said eagerly. "My father's brother fell in love with an American girl and settled over there. No one has seen my uncle or my cousin since she was a small girl. It's the first time I've gotten to meet her!"

"Well, perhaps you can spend the weekend with your family in Athens next week. Get to know your cousin a bit better."

Lisa brightened. "I would like that, Dr. Moustakas."

He nodded and shut the door. As he walked through the cobbled streets, he saw the little village at the edge of the sea where his *yia-yia* had lived was coming alive, and that the ferry boat from the mainland sat at the docks as people boarded it for the hour's jaunt to the mainland and the docks at Piraeus.

It wasn't too much farther to the clinic, and there was a bit of a spring in his step as he headed there. It felt good to be working again and helping out Ares, Theo and Deakin, his best friends, as well as their significant others—he was still having a hard time wrapping his mind around that.

All his friends were matched up. They'd finally found love. He was the only single one left among them. And that wasn't going to change anytime soon. No way.

There had been only one woman he'd come even close to *thinking* about marrying, but he'd bungled that so badly that he'd broken her heart. He deserved to be alone. That was his punishment for the pain he'd caused her. One he'd bear gladly.

Chris sighed and opened the door to the clinic. No one was at the front desk, but the door had been unlocked.

"Ares?" he shouted. There was no answer. "Ares, where are you? Hello?"

"Good gravy, what is with all the *shouting*? I'm coming!" a soft Tennessee accent answered back. One that he knew so well.

His heart skipped a beat as the owner of the voice came charging out of the back of the clinic, dressed to the nines in business attire—the high heels that he'd always thought were ridiculous and a pristine white lab coat.

Her thick strawberry blond hair was swept up off her neck in a tight bun, which didn't suit her, and her soft hazel eyes widened in shock as she froze to the spot.

"Naomi?" he said in a daze as he found his voice. "What're you doing here?"

Oh, my good Lord, what is he doing here?

She knew that Dr. Christos Moustakas was Greek, but she'd had no idea that he was here in Mythelios. She'd thought he was still in Manhattan, playing all-knowing neurosurgical God and playboy.

She'd thought when she left him behind and started working for an international relief effort as a surgeon that she would never have to lay eyes on him again, and that had been good enough for her.

She'd given up so much to take a chance on love and she'd been rejected. He'd shattered her heart and soul three years ago, and she'd never wanted to see him again. *Ever.*

That's not completely true.

She had longed to see him, but she just hadn't been able to risk him hurting her again. Not when it had taken her so long to put her heart back together after he'd so coldly dismissed her—and then she'd lost their baby. The baby she hadn't even known about until after he'd left for New York.

She'd tried to tell him, but he hadn't returned her calls.

So she'd borne that pain alone.

She hated him. He was the reason she didn't date anyone—ever. She'd put her career first because she was never going to make that mistake again.

Her heart was hardened.

You don't hate him. Not really.

Yet here he was. Standing in front of her in clinic scrubs and looking just as good as the day he'd left her all those years ago. His thick dark hair still perfect.

Those dark eyes still with that twinkle in them. And even though he wasn't smiling, just seeing his chiseled handsome face made her go weak in the knees all over again.

No. Don't let him have any power over you.

It had taken her a long time to get over Christos after he'd put his career over her. She'd made her peace with that, and even though she'd blown her chance with Mayo, she'd never blown another one.

And now she was one of the attending surgeons with International Relief. She had a lot of responsibility. Maybe she had him to thank for that—for focusing her mind on her career instead of on him.

Still, she was not happy he was here. Of all the places in the world, why did he have to be here in Mythelios?

Good gravy, why did he have to be here?

She'd been assigned to work between Athens and Mythelios as a surgeon for the next couple of months. When she'd come to Athens in July, she'd gone to the clinic a couple of times, and Chris hadn't been there. Of course, during the first part of her assignment in Greece, she hadn't spent a lot of time in Mythelios, since most of the seriously wounded from the earthquake had been sent to Athens.

And now that she was going to be spending more of her time lending a hand at the clinic, rather than working in the city, he was here—and he was in scrubs as if he belonged here.

You haven't said one word since he asked you what you're doing here. Speak!

"What're *you* doing here?" she asked.

Oh, my Lord in heaven, that was the most pathetic...

She cringed inwardly, because she really didn't know what else to say.

"This is where I'm from. I've come back here because my grandmother died and I inherited her home. Also, this is the clinic I helped found with a few friends of mine. I thought since I was here I would spend some time working here."

"I've been in Greece since last month and I haven't seen you here at the clinic before—and you haven't been mentioned by anyone," she said.

"I've been busy dealing with the passing of my grandmother."

"I had no idea you were from here."

"We didn't do much talking when we were together." There was a twinkle in his eye as he said that.

She groaned. *Of course...* She quickly jogged through all those memories—which were mostly of hot, passion-filled nights. He had once mentioned coming from a small Greek island and helping to found a charitable clinic, but of all the charitable clinics in all of Greece why did she have to walk into *this* one?

It's simple. You're cursed.

That was what her father's mother had said, the one and only time she'd met her when she was fourteen. She'd told her that she was cursed by the gods because she had forsaken her father's heritage and was doomed.

Naomi hadn't given it much credence then, but after meeting Dr. Christos Moustakas four years ago, and having her heart completely trampled on a bare year later, she was beginning to believe her grandmother's words.

She was cursed.

And this just proved it.

"I work with International Relief. I'm here to help on the island after the earthquake. Mythelios and Athens is my assignment for the next couple of months. I'm a general surgeon, and I also raise funds to cover the cost of surgeries for those who can't afford it. The earthquake's damage is wreaking havoc on people."

A smug grin spread across his face. "Is that so? I hadn't heard that."

"Yes," she said firmly, annoyed with him. She clutched the file she was holding tight to her chest. "Dr. Nikolaides did mention to me that a new surgeon would be coming today, but he didn't mention it was you."

"Would that have made a difference?" he asked.

"Yes, of course it would! I'm not happy about this, Dr. Moustakas."

You're supposed to be in New York.

Out of sight and out of mind. Except that was easier said than done. He'd completely crushed her heart. She didn't trust men anymore, thanks to him.

She'd been head over heels in love with Chris. He'd even gotten her pregnant. But he'd made it clear that his career was more important to him than she could ever be. He'd broken things off, and although she'd tried to contact him to tell him about the baby, she'd lost it only a few short weeks after he'd left for New York.

It had destroyed her.

She'd been alone, heartbroken and mad at herself for getting involved with Chris in the first place when she'd known that he'd never wanted anything serious. She'd fallen for his charms. She'd been a fool.

It had taken her this long to pick herself up. To put herself back together. Seeing him again was the very last thing she needed, but it was clear that he was going to stay here and she was just going to have to suck it up and work in the same physical space with him. But that didn't mean they had to work together.

This island was big enough for the both of them.

Oh, who are you kidding?

"Well," Chris said, breaking the tense silence and running a hand through his hair, "I'm sorry that you're not happy about this, Naomi…"

"Dr. Hudson."

"What?" he asked, dazed, and for the first time she noticed the dark circles under his eyes, as if he hadn't been sleeping.

"Dr. Hudson is how I wish to be referred to by you. We're not on a first-name basis. Not anymore."

His eyes narrowed and he frowned, crossing his arms.

He was annoyed by that.

Good.

"Fine. Dr. Hudson, do you think we can work together and remain professional?"

"Of course we can, Dr. Moustakas."

She was relieved—or she should be relieved. Except that she wasn't. Not really.

This is what you want, remember?

"Good, because I really am exhausted and I don't have the energy for games. I've had enough games to last a lifetime."

Her blood boiled and she could feel a flush rise in her cheeks. "I'm very aware of your *games*, Dr. Moustakas. Trust me."

"I don't have time for this," he snapped. He pushed past her and headed to the back where the staff room was. "I need coffee."

She turned and followed him, feeling bad. He was in the back lounge, pouring himself a cup of coffee. He rolled his eyes and groaned when he saw that she'd followed him.

"I'm sorry," she said tentatively.

He eyed her cautiously and took a sip of coffee.

"Why are you so tired?" she asked.

"No reason. Late night," he said quickly, not looking at her.

She knew he was hiding something. This was how he'd acted with her when he'd been given that job offer in Manhattan for an attending position. He would get self-protective—surly, even—and would feign exhaustion as he closed up tight.

She had no time to deal with this. So much was on her plate—including a bachelor auction she had to organize. Originally it had been planned by the clinic as a small affair on Mythelios, to raise funds for the clinic. But when Theo had realized the extent of the damage done by the earthquake to the entire island, he'd suggested to Naomi on her arrival that with her fund-raising background she should take the project on, on behalf of International Relief, and expand it to a much bigger event for maximum exposure and funds.

Having witnessed the desperate need for funds firsthand, Naomi had had no choice but to agree. The auction was now happening in Athens, in a little less than two weeks' time, so she couldn't afford to play Chris's games.

"Well, I'll let you get on with it, then," she said as she backed out of the lounge and made her way to a small office where she could do her paperwork in relative peace.

Maybe she should cancel lunch with her cousin Lisa, who was working on the island as a nanny, and catch an earlier ferry back to Athens. Then at least she'd have the sea to separate herself from Christos Moustakas.

Only, deep down, she knew the sea wasn't enough to keep him at bay. She closed her eyes and tried not to think about Chris and their lost baby, but it all came rushing back to her regardless.

Work was the only thing that kept the pain at bay, but she wasn't sure even that would be enough now, because Chris was here in Mythelios—and he clearly still had the ability to invade both her dreams and her heart.

CHAPTER TWO

CHRIS MANAGED TO avoid Naomi for most of the morning by retreating into one of the offices to go over the file that Ares wanted an opinion on.

He leaned over the computer and frowned as the scans from the Athens MRI came up. The scans were of a local Mythelios bartender whom they all knew and loved.

He'd heard that since the earthquake in May Stavros had been experiencing debilitating headaches, but he'd always brushed them off until finally, the other day, he'd collapsed.

Now Chris knew why Stavros had been having such a hard time, because he was staring down at one of the biggest anaplastic oligodendrogliomas that he'd ever seen.

Dammit.

He knew men like Stavros; the older generation of men from the island were stubborn and brushed off what they thought were minor symptoms, like a headache, as nothing. "Minor symptoms" that might be warning them of something far more sinister. Like Stavros's headaches.

Chris leaned back in the swivel chair and scrubbed

a hand over his face in frustration. This surgery would be intricate and costly.

It was too expensive to have the clinic cover the cost—especially since the clinic was still trying to recover financially from the consequences of the earthquake. And even though Stavros had a successful *taverna*, Chris was pretty sure that he didn't have enough money to pay for this surgery.

Yet Chris couldn't let him die. He had to try to find a way to help Stavros. He had to get a surgical team together. He needed an operating room and post-anesthesia care. The list was endless.

He hated cases like this, but he also loved cases like this. It was a challenge, and he hadn't had a challenge like this in so long.

"That's one nasty-looking tumor," Naomi said, interrupting his thoughts.

Chris turned to see Naomi leaning in the doorway, her eyes fixed on the screen. She was so close to him he could smell the sweet scent of her perfume. Jasmine and magnolia. It reminded him of his time in Nashville. The flowers from the trees there had bloomed and filled the air with their sweet fragrance, and every time he'd taken Naomi in his arms he'd thought of those flowers. The blooms so soft, so delicate and so beautiful…

Get a hold of yourself.

"Yes. It is. A local patient who hasn't got time to wait for a place on a state-provided health care surgery list. To pay privately it's going to be costly, and I don't think he'll be able to afford it, sadly. If he wants to live, I'm going to have to get him to Athens and do it myself."

Which made him think about how he'd have to uproot Evangelos and take him to Athens too. He would have to find a big enough rental unit so that he, Lisa and Evangelos all had their privacy. It was going to be a nightmare, but Chris couldn't sit back and do nothing. Stavros would die.

"Well, you know the International Relief effort might be willing to help this patient out."

"I thought those funds could only be used to help out earthquake victims. He might have been a victim of the earthquake, but this tumor has been growing for several years."

"Funds are to help those in need," she said. "If he needs help—"

"I have to talk to the patient first and give him all the details," Chris interrupted. "He may say no."

"Yes, but you're saying he needs the surgery. Correct?" she asked.

"Yes. He does."

"Do you know him? Do you think he'll agree to the surgery?"

"Only if he gets to pay his way. He's stubborn—like most men from this island."

He couldn't help but grin at her, and for a brief moment he thought he saw a flicker of humor in her eyes and a small twitch of a smile on her lips.

"Well, I'll try to find out more information. I would like to help in any way that I can. I used to…"

She trailed off and the pink flush of a blush bloomed in her cheeks. He knew what she was going to say, because he was thinking it too.

"You used to assist me in surgery. You were a brilliant neurosurgical resident. Please tell me you didn't give up neurosurgery."

"Oh, you mean *after* you got the fellowship and then the position in Manhattan?"

Chris sighed. "I didn't take that position to hurt you, Naomi."

She frowned. "I know that—and, yes, I'm still a neurosurgeon, as well as a more than competent general surgeon, which was what was particularly needed in the aftermath of the earthquake."

"I'm glad."

And he was. Naomi was far too talented to be wasted.

He had been so relieved when he'd gotten that position in New York. Naomi had been getting way too close to him for comfort. She'd become part of his life in a way he'd never wanted a woman to be. The Manhattan job had been an escape and he'd jumped at the chance.

He'd completed his fellowship and then become an attending all within three years, and he didn't regret it. The only thing he regretted was losing her along the way. Being so scared of committing to one woman for the rest of his life that he'd run away rather than face up to his fears.

And he regretted hurting her career. He wanted to ask her about whether she'd ever got into Mayo. He wanted to know what she'd done after they'd parted. But he couldn't find the words. He was still far too ashamed.

He glanced at his watch.

It was noon, and he had to head back to relieve Lisa for lunch. Besides, he wouldn't mind having a light lunch at home and a quick nap. The coffee, though strong, had not woken him up. He needed sleep.

"Well, I'd better get some lunch." He stood. "Are you eating here?"

"No, I have plans. A lunch date," she said.

A lunch date? With who?

He was surprised by the sharp burst of jealousy that reared its ugly head deep inside him.

You don't have any claim on her now.

"Oh…?"

"Yes," she said noncommittally, not taking the bait and elaborating. "So, I'll see you later, back at the clinic?"

"Yeah. Enjoy your lunch date."

"Oh, I will," she chirped.

Follow her. Find out who he is.

Only, he wasn't going to do that. He wasn't going to let that jealous, foolish part of him take over. It had been way too many years since he'd gotten into any kind of a brawl over a girl, and he couldn't afford to have his hands out of commission now. Not when he had to get Stavros over to Athens as soon as possible and get that tumor out of him.

Theo was in the hall, waiting for the computer when he left.

"You done?" Theo asked.

"Yeah."

"You okay?"

No. But he didn't say that out loud. He'd never told his friends about Naomi and he wasn't going to elaborate on that secret shame now.

"I just need a nap. Babies are bad for sleep," Chris teased. "You'll see soon enough."

"Great. I can't wait." Theo grinned.

"Hey, is Stavros coming in again today?" Chris asked.

"No, he's working." Theo frowned. "Is this about those scans?"

"He has a very aggressive brain tumor. I have to get him to Athens and do a *very* expensive surgery."

"He's not going to like that," Theo commented. "He never leaves his *taverna*. He's not going to agree to surgery unless it can be done here on the island and he can be back to work in an hour or less."

Chris laughed at that. "Well, none of that's going to happen."

"The surgery could happen here if necessary."

"Theo, I'd need a surgical team that's used to operating on grade three anaplastic oligodendrogliomas. I also think he's going to need some chemotherapy afterward. And I'll need more scans to see if the cancer has progressed."

"I can tell you now—Stavros won't leave Mythelios. You're going to have to work a miracle," Theo announced, ducking into the office and leaving Chris cursing under his breath.

Why did the men on this island feel they needed to be pigheaded and stubborn to the point at which it cost them everything? Stavros with his brain cancer... his father driving his mother away...and him doing exactly the same thing to Naomi because he'd taken the New York job without consulting her. He'd just upped and left.

Maybe he was cursed?

On days like today it didn't feel as if he had any kind of blessing from the gods smiling down on him. Not that the patron saint of Mythelios had smiled on him in a long time.

What about Evangelos?

Chris's bad attitude melted away.

Yeah, there was Evan. Chris might not have the love of a woman, but he had his son to brighten his life.

And that was all he needed.

"I'm headed for lunch, Theo," Chris called over his shoulder.

"See you," Theo called back.

Chris ducked out the back door and headed along the faster route, through the winding streets to his *yia-yia's* home. He'd just slipped off his shoes when there was a knock at the front door.

Lisa came down the stairs. "That's my cousin. I'm meeting her for lunch. I'm just finishing feeding Evan and then I'll be there."

Chris nodded. "Take your time. I'll let her know."

Lisa nodded and headed back upstairs to where Evangelos was hollering for strained peas—quite loudly.

Chris opened the door.

"Sorry I'm late, I got lost," the woman outside began breathlessly. "I— *Chris?*"

"Hi, Naomi. So you're Lisa's cousin."

He mentally rolled his eyes at the gods, who were surely laughing at him now.

Just. Great. What's he doing here? Can't I get away from him?

"This is where my cousin works. I thought you were…" Then she trailed off as she realized. "This is your home?"

He nodded. "It is. You'd better come in."

Naomi stepped over the threshold and he shut the wooden door to help keep the heat out of the house. She'd seen this house when she'd first arrived on Mythelios. It was on the topmost part of the hill and it overlooked the sea. It was brilliant white, surrounded by the bright colors of the other houses. It had a huge balcony, and she'd imagined what it would be like to live there. To always see the sea.

She'd wondered about the family who lived there. Her cousin hadn't said much about the people she worked for. Only that it was a family with money and that her charge was a young baby.

Baby? But Chris lives here.

Of course he'd found someone else. Of course he was married now. *His* heart hadn't been broken when things had ended between them.

She remembered hearing about all the women he'd been with. He was a playboy in Manhattan, regularly seen out and about with a variety of famous women. And he had money, so of course he would be married.

"My cousin is a nanny," she stated, feeling foolish.

"Yes. I'm aware of that," he said, and his mouth quirked up in a half smile—the one that had always made her melt in the past. "It's my son she cares for when I'm working."

"*Your* son?"

"Yes," he said. "My son, Evangelos. He's eight months old now."

"What about his mother?" Naomi asked.

"My, you're full of questions today," he teased.

"I'm sorry. I just… You were always very clear that you never wanted a wife or kids. You didn't want a family."

"I don't understand. Why can't I come to New York with you?"

"You don't have a position there."

"So? I want to be with you."

His muscles had tensed and she'd seen a look that had made her stomach churn.

"You knew this wasn't long-term. I don't want marriage. I don't want a wife or kids. Don't follow me, Naomi. Don't waste your life pursuing me when I can't give you what you want."

"Circumstances changed," he said now.

Yes, because I wasn't the right woman for you.

And her heart ached as she thought about the baby— *their* baby—the one she had lost. She would have loved that child. She'd always wanted children.

So Chris had got that too.

"Well, I'm happy for you and your wife."

"I'm not married, Naomi. Not much has changed on that score. I have a son, yes, but no wife. Evan was the result of a one-night stand with a woman who just wanted me for the money. She was going to get rid of the child unless I paid her quite a lot of money to have him. I didn't want her to get rid of him, so...here I am. A single father."

Lisa came down the stairs and in her arms was a baby.

Naomi was struck by how much the little boy looked like Chris. Same dark eyes and hair, but the little boy had the biggest cheeks she'd ever seen, and a gummy smile that completely lit up his face when he saw Chris.

"Sorry," Lisa said, handing the baby over to Chris. "He got up late and then his whole schedule was thrown off."

"It's okay," Chris said. "Enjoy lunch with your cousin. I'll see you back here in an hour."

Chris then turned his entire focus onto his son as he carried him up the stairs away from the hallway. The baby gurgled and laughed, and all Naomi could do was stand there in stunned silence.

Her heart was melting as she watched how loving he was with his son.

And thought how completely heartbroken it made her feel.

CHAPTER THREE

SHE COULDN'T GET the picture of Chris carrying his son up the stairs out of her mind. How he'd held the baby so close and just how much he'd doted on him.

Would he have doted on *their* baby just as much?

She wanted to think he would, but she couldn't be sure, and the fact that they would never know made her sad. Made her ache.

It had been a long time since she'd let herself think about her baby and the miscarriage. She never let her mind go there...it was too painful.

Work usually took care of that, but now she was working with Chris and he constantly reminded her of what might have been. What she might have had.

"You're awfully quiet, Naomi," Lisa said, interrupting Naomi's thoughts.

"What?"

"I said you're quiet," Lisa teased. "I thought you were a chatterbox when we first met."

"Sorry. I've got a lot on my mind." Naomi fidgeted with her napkin and tried to put Chris and his son out of her mind—but she couldn't.

She just saw him again and again in her mind's eye, kissing that baby who was the spitting image of him.

"I noticed. You've completely missed those handsome men over there who have been trying to get your attention for some time."

Naomi turned and glanced over at the men in question. They were young—around Lisa's age, which was about eight years her junior. They were definitely flirting with them, but Naomi wasn't interested.

"Did you know your father's mother? Our *yia-yia*?"

Lisa frowned. "Not really. She died when I was about seven years old. She lived outside of Athens and we rarely went to see her. She hated my mother. And *Yia-yia* travelled a lot. She died shortly after she came back from America."

"She used to say I was cursed." Naomi laughed half-heartedly.

Lisa looked confused. "Cursed? What? You were like...what...? Fourteen when you met her?"

Naomi nodded. "Yep—and she called me cursed or the cursed one the entire time she was visiting. Really annoyed my mother and father."

"Well, my father said that *Yia-yia* had that effect on people. I don't think you're cursed, and I definitely don't believe in curses, but people around here do take religion seriously. When they bring out the Saint for his yearly airing, people are really into seeing his mummified remains being carted around in a gold sarcophagus. They say it brings good luck, but I don't know..."

"I could use some good luck," Naomi said, and groaned. "This bachelor auction is coming up fast at the end of the month. It's being held in Athens now, rather than on Mythelios, so we can get more exposure and hopefully more funds for the wider community as well as the clinic. Theo thought I was the perfect person to take it on, and it's a great idea, but now I have to find some bachelors from Mythelios to auction off.

Bachelors who are willing to give a romantic fantasy type of date. I was hoping to coerce some of the male doctors here into it, but they all *have* someone."

Lisa took a sip of her iced tea. "There's always my boss. He's single. He has a baby, but it's just a date for charity. It's not like you're selling off husbands or something. I'm sure if he knew what it was for he'd say yes. He's quite generous."

I'm sure.

"I'm sure he has enough women on his hands that he doesn't need to be auctioned off."

Lisa frowned. "Actually, no, I've never seen him on a date. He's totally devoted to his son and his work. Mind you, I've only known him since I was hired to care for Evan. I don't remember him from when my family would visit the island when I was a child."

"Do you know anything about the baby's mother?"

Lisa frowned. "Nothing. I just know that she's not in the picture and that Chris has full custody of his son. Which is why he hired me shortly after he returned to Greece a few weeks ago. The only woman who lived with him before I came was Dr. Erianthe Nikolaides, but not for long. She's married to Dr. Xenakis now."

Naomi worried at her bottom lip, because she couldn't help but wonder what kind of woman Evan's mother was. Why didn't she want her baby?

Naomi would've given anything to keep *her* baby.

One thing she knew: she felt really sorry for that sweet little boy, growing up without a mother.

"I can't ask Dr. Moustakas to take part in the bachelor auction," she said, steering the subject back to the auction because she didn't want to think about Chris and his baby. How it had made her completely weak in the knees to see them together.

She'd never seen him like that before. So gentle, so loving. It made her long for what had been taken from her. For what she'd never got to have.

"You *can* ask Dr. Moustakas. He'll probably say yes—and, honestly, he needs a night away," Lisa said. "He really has no life."

Lisa continued to chat about different things, but Naomi was only half listening. It surprised her to hear that Chris had become something of a hermit when he'd been the quintessential playboy in Manhattan—or so all the tabloids had said, when she was doing her fellowship in Nashville.

The church bell in the center of the old town chimed the hour.

"I'd better get back. Evangelos is due for a walk and Dr. Moustakas has to get back to work." Lisa picked up her shawl and purse. "Are you heading back to Athens tonight?"

Naomi nodded. "There's no place to stay on the island after the earthquake—though Dr. Nikolaides did offer a boathouse. But a place like that is more suited to a bachelor. Are you headed back to Athens too?"

"No, I'm on for three nights and then off for two. I have a small room close to Evangelos. I suppose when the boy gets older I'll be making the commute daily, but it's really not that long."

"No, but it would be easier to stay here. Isn't there a ferry that goes to Spritos?"

Lisa frowned. "Spritos? What do you need to do there?"

"There's another small clinic there, and I was told Spritos could be accessed by ferry from Mythelios."

"On the other side of the island. The ferry only runs twice a day. Once in the morning and once in the evening. Pray you don't get stuck there, because they really have nothing—but it's a beautiful place."

Naomi walked Lisa back to Chris's house.

"I hope we can visit more," Lisa said as she unlocked the old wooden door to Chris's home. "It's nice that you're here, and if *Yia-yia* did put a curse on you, perhaps we can lift it, eh?"

Naomi laughed. "I would like that."

She turned and began walking back to the clinic. She made slow progress and was annoyed with herself for wearing completely impractical heels—especially when walking on cobbled streets. Then her heel broke, and she swore out loud and leaned precariously against a wall to inspect the damage.

Yep. Definitely cursed.

There was the beep of a horn behind her, and she looked over her shoulder to see a little scooter being driven by none other than Chris, who was grinning from ear to ear as he leaned over the front.

"I told you those heels would be your downfall one day."

She snorted. "I wasn't thinking. In Athens it's no big deal."

"Here, especially on the cobbled streets of the old part of town, flats are your friend. How badly is it broken?"

"Bad—but I do have a pair of flip-flops in my bag back at the clinic. I was planning on getting a pedicure in Athens when I returned tonight."

"Well, you won't make it hobbling like that. Do you want a ride to the clinic?"

She eyed the scooter speculatively. "I thought you walked."

"In the morning, yes, but I'm running late and I

thought I'd take this for a spin. It was my *yia-yia's* and is proving handy."

"Your *yia-yia's*?" Naomi tried to picture a tiny little grandmother, dressed in black, motoring around Mythelios on this little turquoise scooter.

"Why not?"

"A scooter's not very practical for a man with a baby."

"I have a car on the mainland. The ferry's not a far walk and neither is the clinic. Do you want a ride or do you want to spend all day holding up that wall?"

"Thanks."

Naomi hobbled over to him and climbed precariously onto the back of the scooter, sitting sidesaddle behind him because she was wearing a tight pencil skirt. She crossed her legs at the ankles.

He glanced over his shoulder at her. "Uh…you do have to hold on."

"There's nothing to hold on to."

"Sure there is. Me. You have to hold on to *me*."

Definitely cursed.

"Fine," she murmured as she slipped her arms around his waist.

Under his loose scrubs she could feel every single one of his abdominal muscles, and when she closed her eyes, she could see him without his shirt on and it made her heart beat just a little bit faster.

She'd never really forgotten the electric effect he'd had on her, and being so close to him now, with her body pressed against his, it all came rushing back, making her blood heat and her palms sweat.

She hated that he still had this effect on her. Why *did* he still have this effect on her? Why was she letting him get to her?

Because you're weak. Because you've never really gotten over him.

"You ready?"

"No!" she said, but nodded.

He chuckled. "Hang on."

Chris revved the engine and the little scooter took off down the hill, through the narrow cobbled streets of the old part of Mythelios. Naomi closed her eyes tight for a few moments as Chris drove like a maniac through the streets, but then he turned away from the clinic road onto another road. A dirt track that overlooked the sea.

"Where are we going?" she shrieked over the roar of the engine.

"Just taking the back way," he teased. "A more scenic route, since you probably haven't seen all of Mythelios yet."

"Uh, no—I really need to get back."

"Live a little, Naomi. You're always so uptight."

That was what he'd said to her when they'd first met, and look where that had gotten her. It had left her with a broken heart, an unimaginable loss and, for the first time in her life, without a clue as to how to go on.

She'd fought hard to dig herself out of that pit of heartbreak and learn to put herself first. She wasn't going to let him do that to her again.

"Chris, stop this thing *now*!"

Chris pulled over into a lay-by and stopped the scooter. Once she was off, she slipped off her shoes and began to walk barefoot down the dirt track toward the clinic.

"Naomi, I was only joking."

She spun around. "That's the thing. You're always *joking*! I have *real* work to do. I have patients to see this afternoon! I don't have time to waste driving all over the island just because I need to let loose! I've done enough of that in my life and look where it got me."

Tears were stinging her eyes—not because she was sad, but because she always cried when she got mad, and she was mad about this whole situation. How he thought things could ever be normal between them was a mystery to her.

Maybe she was cursed and maybe he had all the luck, but she worked hard for what she wanted, for what she'd achieved, and she wasn't going to let him stand in her way this time.

"Naomi!" he called out, but she ignored him, limping along the road, feeling small pebbles digging into the soles of her feet.

Chris came jogging up beside her and took her hand in his. It was so strong, so warm.

"I'm sorry, Naomi."

There was sincerity in his eyes, and a well of sadness.

"Please let me take you back to the clinic and I'll make it up to you any way that I can."

"You'll make it up to me?" she asked.

He nodded. "Of course. I was impertinent and flippant and I'll do whatever it takes to make things right. I'll do whatever it takes to make this whole thing go away so we can work together."

"Okay." She grinned suddenly. "I know *exactly* how you can make it up to me."

He cocked a wary eyebrow. "Really? That fast?"

"Yes. It's something that's put me in a bit of a predicament."

"What is it?" Chris asked hesitantly.

"*You're* going to be my feature bachelor."

His expression fell. "What?"

"At a charity auction to raise money for earthquake

relief. You're going to give up your time and take the highest bidder on a romantic night out."

He wasn't quite sure that he'd heard her right.

"You want me to do *what*?" he asked in disbelief.

"Be in the bachelor auction."

"No way!" he almost shouted at her, throwing up his arms.

"You said you'd make it up to me, and being the featured bachelor in our Hot Greek Nights bachelor auction would definitely be a highlight."

"Nope." He shook his head and crossed his arms. "I'm not a bachelor."

A strange expression crossed her face and for a fleeting moment he thought he saw that flare of jealousy again.

"You're involved with someone?" she asked slowly.

"No, but…"

She held up her hand to silence him. "Then you're doing it, pal."

"I think not. I'm a single father. I don't have time to do a charity auction."

"Even if it will help those less fortunate here in Mythelios? Those who were affected by the earthquake? Not everyone is so lucky as to have a trust fund and live like you do. There are other single parents out there seriously struggling to survive."

Dammit.

He couldn't argue with that, and if it was to help out with fund-raising, there was no way he could walk away from it. Naomi had him cornered, the minx.

"Who suggested me?" he grumbled.

"No one did. I see no wedding band. Like you said, you're a single father."

"I told you my son's mother made it clear that she did not want him and left," he snapped, surprised at how touchy he was about it.

"I'm sorry it didn't work out."

"There was nothing *to* work out. I told you it was a one-night stand. I regret sleeping with Evan's biological mother, but I don't regret having him in my life."

An unreadable expression crossed her face and he couldn't quite place it, but then it vanished again as quickly as it had appeared.

"So, will you do it?"

He ran a hand through his hair. "I guess I have no choice—because I can't have you cut your feet up walking back down to the clinic, nor have you savaged by a wandering goat." A smile tugged at the corner of his mouth when he saw her eyes widen.

"Goats?"

He laughed. "I'll do it. What do I need to do, though?"

"Just think of something romantic to do with whoever wins the date. You were always pretty good at that."

A blush rose in her cheeks and his blood heated. He loved it when she blushed, and it made him feel good that he still had some kind of effect on her after all this time.

She was the only woman he'd ever cared about. Even though he'd been completely stubborn and too pigheaded back then to see it.

And now it was too late.

Is it?

"Come on, let's get you back to the clinic," he said, heading back to the scooter.

"Before I'm savaged by a goat?" she teased.

"Yeah."

Naomi stumbled over some of the small rocks on this

section of the road and without thinking he closed the distance between them and scooped her up, carrying her the short distance back to the scooter.

She was blushing again.

"This…" she whispered as he sat her down on the back of the scooter.

"What?"

"Sweep the winner off her feet. You're good at that too."

"Okay. I'll think of something." He climbed onto the scooter.

"Thank you, by the way. In case I don't say it later. You're making my life just a bit easier," she said gently.

He smiled. "You're welcome."

He fired up the scooter and made a careful turn off the winding hill road. Her arms were around him again and it felt so right. She'd told him that he was good at sweeping a woman off her feet, and perhaps he was, but there was only ever one woman whom he'd truly wanted to do that to and she was sitting behind him.

And she didn't want him anymore.

CHAPTER FOUR

"You're daydreaming again, eh?"

Chris looked up to see Ares standing over him. Ares had a mischievous glint in his dark eyes as he sat down next to Chris in the clinic's lounge.

"I wasn't daydreaming. I might've been nodding off, though. I have a young son and I don't get much sleep, so I tend to zone out."

Ares snorted. "Sure, that must be it. It has nothing to do with Dr. Hudson."

Chris straightened his spine and sat up. "What're you talking about?"

"I see the way you look at her and the way she acts around you. Is she one of your paramours from America?"

No, she was more than that. But he'd been too much of a coward back then to do anything about it.

Ares didn't need to know that.

"Something like that..." Chris stretched.

"Why didn't you tell us? If you'd told us, we could've had someone else from International Relief come in her place," Ares said.

"No, don't do that—it's not necessary." Chris sighed. "It was nothing, and we're still friends."

Ares cocked an eyebrow and Chris could tell that he didn't believe him.

"You're sure you don't want to talk about it?"

"Yes, I'm sure."

Chris didn't want to talk about Naomi with Ares, Deakin or Theo. He didn't want them to think badly of him—the way he felt about himself for walking away from her.

"I heard that you're now the lone bachelor representing us in that bachelor auction in Athens in a couple of weeks. Thanks for doing that, but I seriously doubt that you'll earn as much money as I would have."

Chris snorted. "*You* were supposed to be the feature bachelor?"

"What's with the snort of derision? Of *course*. No woman can resist me or my charms." Ares grinned and tossed his head, making those long dark curls bounce.

Chris rolled his eyes. "Don't let Erianthe hear you talking like that."

"Right," Ares said, chuckling.

"So what were you going to do?" Chris asked.

"I was going to walk across the stage in a tuxedo," Ares answered, puzzled.

Chris punched him in the arm. "No, I meant for the date. What were you going to do? What's romantic in Greece? I'm too used to sweeping a girl off her feet in Manhattan. I think I'm out of touch."

And *that* was the understatement of the year. He was definitely out of touch—and had been since the day Evan's mother had told him she was pregnant. That was when his life had come to a screeching halt.

It was also the night when he'd stopped sleeping soundly.

"Well, I was planning on hiring a yacht and taking

the lucky winner out on a moonlight boat ride. Spritos isn't far, and my plan was to have a little impromptu fancy picnic set up on one of the beaches your father owns, complete with a waiter and the very best champagne. Maybe some dancing under the stars."

"You're quite the Valentino, Ares."

Ares grinned. "I know."

"Well, that might be going a bit overboard." Chris rolled his shoulders to loosen the tension knot that had formed in his back. "I'm not trying to seduce the woman. Just give her her money's worth."

"Oh, for sure—because *your* seduction technique would have her demanding a refund."

Ares got up and jogged out of the room before Chris could react.

Yeah, you'd better run!

Ares's idea wasn't half-bad, though. His father had a yacht he could use, and Chris was pretty sure that the captain who ran it would do the tour pro bono, but since his father's yacht was a bit larger than what Ares had planned, dinner on the beach was probably a bit out of reach.

What was he doing?

He should have just said no to being in the auction!

Actually, he shouldn't have done such a spur-of-the-moment thing and taken Naomi on that scooter ride at all. He didn't know what had come over him.

Exhaustion. That's what your problem is.

Or guilt. Naomi could have asked him for almost anything and he'd have given it to her.

Except marriage. You couldn't give her that.

Chris swore under his breath as he tried to forget about that. He couldn't be thinking about that now, when he had a patient to see.

Deakin poked his head into the lounge. "Stavros is here for his appointment."

He wasn't looking forward to this, but it had to be done.

"Thanks, Deakin."

"He's in exam room one." Deakin left and Chris picked up his notebook.

How did you tell someone he was dying? He'd never get used to telling patients that. In Manhattan he had all the newest equipment and the finest surgical team at his fingertips, but here in a small island clinic he was feeling distinctly uneasy.

Even if Stavros agreed to go to Athens, the neuro-surgical team there wasn't *his*. They wouldn't be used to his nuances, and that upped the risk factor of this whole thing.

Chris gathered up Stavros's file and headed to exam room one. He knocked on the door and slipped in when Stavros responded.

"So the prodigal son returns to Mythelios," Stavros said brightly. "Your *yia-yia* was a regular at my *taverna*. She was a force to be reckoned with, God rest her soul."

Chris nodded. "That she was."

"You've only been to my *taverna* once, though, since you came home."

"I've been busy. And I have a young son."

"Ah, well, congratulations. I hadn't heard," Stavros said.

Only, Chris was pretty sure that Stavros had heard. Stavros knew everything, and this forgetfulness might be the tumor talking.

"Thank you."

Stavros smiled. "So I take it since they brought in such a big gun to handle my file after the headaches and the seizure, that it's something a bit more serious than epilepsy?"

Chris nodded solemnly. "I'm sorry, Stavros, but you have a grade three anaplastic oligodendroglioma. It's a fast-growing, rare and aggressive form of tumor that is growing in your temporal lobe. If left untreated, it will spread to other parts of your body."

"What're my options?" Stavros asked calmly.

"I would like to get some more scans to see if the cancer has spread anywhere else first, and then I can form a plan of attack. But ideally I would operate to remove what I can and then give you a course of chemotherapy."

"Chemotherapy?" Stavros shook his head. "But who would run my *taverna*? I can't agree to that—and I doubt I could afford it either."

"Stavros, if you refuse treatment, you'll have maybe six months to live."

"It's a risk I'm willing to take. I can't be so sick that I'm unable to work. The *taverna* is my livelihood, and without it I can't pay for the surgery."

"I'll pay for the surgery."

"With all due respect, Dr. Moustakas, I don't take charity."

"Let me at least do the scans in Athens. I'll set you up an appointment for a Sunday so that it won't affect your work. If it hasn't spread, then you won't have to have chemotherapy. I would just do the operation."

Stavros frowned. "Can I think about it?"

"Of course. I'm really sorry."

"Thank you, Dr. Moustakas. I really appreciate it."

Chris left the exam room and took the file back to the filing cabinet. Naomi was standing next to it, and she cocked one of her finely arched brows when she saw him.

"You look terrible. You okay?" she asked.

"Yeah, I just had to deliver the bad news to Stavros."

Her expression softened. "I'm sorry. How did he take it?"

"He's stubborn, but that's not surprising. He'll come around, but at the moment he's refusing any kind of charity. He wants to pay for surgery on his own—except the surgery will take everything he's saved and probably his *taverna* as well."

"It's pride. I get that. And I'm still trying to find a way to have the relief fund pay for the surgery," she said.

"I don't think he'd accept it. He doesn't want charity, but then again he may take it if it's a last resort. I'm hoping he'll at least agree to go to Athens to have a full body scan, just so I can see if the cancer has spread, because if it has spread, then all I can offer Stavros is comfort measures." He scrubbed a hand over his face. "Do you have an in with the chief of surgery at an Athens hospital?"

"I do. Why?" she asked.

"The only way I can get Stavros to agree to a scan is to have it done on a Sunday, when his *taverna* is closed."

Naomi smiled. "I'll see what I can do."

"Thank you. I appreciate it."

All he wanted to do was go home and sleep, but Naomi lingered and he had a feeling that he wasn't going home anytime soon.

"Why are you looking at me like that?"

She handed him a piece of paper. "Information about the bachelor auction in Athens that you agreed to yesterday. I've already talked to my cousin about watching your son that night."

"I know Lisa is your cousin, but you shouldn't be arranging things with my child's nanny behind my back," he said stiffly.

Even though he was grateful she'd done it, he didn't want her wiggling her way into his life. He didn't want her to get hurt when he couldn't give her what she wanted. He had to protect Evangelos. Chris didn't deserve her kindness or concern.

"I know. I'm sorry. But she was very glad to do it. I confess she's the one who suggested you when I found out that all the other doctors here in the clinic are already spoken for."

"She suggested me, eh?"

He would have to have a talk with her later, but he was glad that Lisa was willing to work an extra night to watch Evan. Chances were that someone from outside Mythelios would win him, and he didn't want anyone to know about his son. His son wouldn't be used as a selling point in this bachelor auction.

"There will be no mention of Evangelos. You can talk about my medical career, and even who my father is, but you will *not* mention at the auction that I am a single parent."

Naomi nodded. "Of course. I understand. So who *is* your father? I always knew you were well-off, but we didn't talk much about our families."

Warmth spread through his body as he thought about what they'd done instead of talking. An image of her in his arms, naked, his hands in her hair as he kissed her over and over, flitted through his mind.

Focus.

"You ever hear of Mopaxeni Shipping?"

She raised her eyebrows. "The big shipping empire? Of course—who *hasn't* heard of it?"

"My father is one of the head figures behind that enterprise. I'm sure just a mention that I am a Mopaxeni heir will drive up the bids."

"Most certainly—but aren't you worried that some fortune-hunting heiress will get her hooks into you and sweep you off your feet?"

She'd meant it as a joke, but it hit a little too close to home and reminded him of Evangelos's mother.

"Give me a million and I'll keep the baby. You can have it, and I'll sign away my rights to it, but a million is my price. As well as an apartment in Central Park West."

"Are you serious?" Chris had shouted.

"Very," Lillian had said coolly. *"I won't have this baby for less than that."*

"What about marriage?" Though he'd cringed inwardly even thinking about that, he'd known it was the right thing to do.

"I don't want marriage. I want money, Chris. If you won't agree to my terms, then I will get rid of this baby."

Chris had clenched his fists. What had he ever seen in her? She was cruel, vicious and greedy.

You did this to yourself, the voice in his head had told him. *You had it all with Naomi and you threw it away. This is your punishment.*

"Fine. I'll agree to your terms and you will relinquish all rights to our child. And you will agree to attending medical appointments and keeping yourself healthy. Doing nothing to jeopardize our child."

"And when will I get my payment?" Lillian had asked.

"Half now and half when the child is born."

He remembered that call to his father, when he'd had to ask for the money to buy the apartment and a check for a million. His father had scolded him about his irresponsible ways and Chris had had to agree with him on that score.

He might be a brilliant neurosurgeon, but when it came to matters of the heart, he was a bit of a fool.

"Don't worry. I won't give them too good of a time," Chris finally said, breaking the tension that had descended between him and Naomi.

"What are your big plans, then?" she asked.

"That's a secret," he replied.

The yacht idea that Ares had suggested was good, but he really didn't know much beyond that.

"I have to know beforehand. The date is sort of pitched as part of the package," she said. "I really hate doing this too, but it's a means to an end."

A smile quirked his lips. He loved it when she got all worked up and her Tennessee accent became thicker.

"I'll let you know as soon as I can."

She nodded and then glanced at her watch. "I'd better go if I'm going to catch the next ferry to Athens."

"Yes—and I should go home and relieve Lisa so she can have her dinner."

No sooner had the words come out of his mouth than there was a shout from the front of the clinic.

"Help! Please! It's my son! He was in a crash and he hit his head—he's unconscious!"

The woman was beside herself.

Chris followed the woman into the street just outside the clinic. A young man had been riding a scooter without a helmet and he'd hit a tree. And from the way he was lying on the road, with his right temple against the stone curb, Chris had no doubt the man would have a concussion.

Naomi knelt down next to him and gently began to examine the young man.

"Airway and breathing is good," she said.

"I need to get him inside," said Chris. "But first I want to assess him for any injury to his spine."

Naomi nodded. "What do you need?"

"Get a backboard and I'll examine him."

She nodded and disappeared back into the clinic as Chris made his preliminary examination. The left pupil was blown, but the right was responsive. The young man was alive, and that was all that mattered.

Naomi returned with the backboard just as Chris finished his examination. Together they gently lifted their patient on. He didn't have to bark orders to Naomi. She knew exactly what was needed, what he wanted to be done as head neurosurgeon. They had always worked well together—which was why he had been so drawn to her when he'd first met her.

There was still something there.

He wasn't blind.

Or could it be that she's also a neurosurgical fellow on top of a general surgeon?

He shook that errant thought away as they strapped the man down and together carried him into the clinic.

Right now he couldn't think about all the *what ifs* and reminisce about working with Naomi. Not now, when a man's life was hanging in the balance.

"Malakas!"

Naomi cringed as she heard Chris curse from the other room. The CT scanner was on the fritz again. She'd been told by Theo that it hadn't been working well since the earthquake, and they urgently needed a new one.

Their patient, Maximos Ponao, was still unconscious,

and Chris was positive that there was a hematoma. There was a definite depressed skull fracture.

"Aha!" Chris shouted triumphantly as the scanner finally fired up. He joined her in the observation room as Maximos was scanned. "If this keeps working like this, I'm going to have Stavros scanned here. An MRI is less invasive, but a CT scan will do just as well."

"That will make Stavros happy," Naomi remarked.

They sat next to each other, waiting for the scanner to send images to the computer.

"What will you do if there is a hematoma? There is an operating room available, and we can call staff back in," she said.

But she was really hoping that Chris wouldn't attempt to evacuate the hematoma and the fracture and would just wait for the air ambulance to land. Once they had Maximos stable, she'd call for the air ambulance from Athens to come and get him.

"Unless he's at death's door, no, I don't want to do brain surgery here," Chris said. "The surgical staff are great, but they're not used to brain surgery and a depressed skull fracture requires a certain finesse. I'm not comfortable doing it here."

"Yet you are the best neurosurgeon in the United States. There's no denying it—you're at the top of the game. This young man could do worse."

Chris's jaw tightened and he didn't look at her. He kept his eyes fixed on the computer screen, but he said, "Thank you."

The images came up and Chris swore under his breath. "I'm glad you called the air ambulance. You can see he has clotted blood along the interhemispheric fissure and he's developing hydrocephalus. He needs surgery at once to relieve the pressure."

"They'll be here soon."

As if on cue they could hear the distant whir of the helicopter as it crossed the few miles between Mythe- lios and mainland Greece.

"I'll go let them in," Naomi said.

She ran as best as she could in the flip-flops that had replaced her broken heels and met the paramedic team as the helicopter landed on the roof. She explained what had happened, and which hospital to take the patient to.

Chris was waiting for them, and he helped the para- medics carry the stretcher up to the roof. The young man's mother followed. She would travel with the air ambulance to the mainland, since the ferry had stopped for the night.

Once Maximos was loaded, Chris put his arm around Naomi as the helicopter's blades came to life, nearly blowing her over. He led her out of their path, back into the doorway, and they watched the helicopter disappear into the inky-black night, its lights flashing as it headed swiftly back to the mainland.

"So, it looks like you lost your only ride back to the mainland tonight," Chris remarked. "And there's already a doctor sleeping in the on-call room."

"It appears so. Well, the couch in the lounge looks comfy enough. I'm sure I'll be fine there for the night."

Though she didn't really relish the idea of trying to curl up on the couch that time had forgotten. It was fine for sitting on, or a short nap, but it really was as hard as a rock.

"Nonsense. You can spend the night with me."

Heat bloomed in her cheeks as she thought of the last time he'd asked her to spend the night with him.

"I want you to spend the night," Chris had whispered against her ear, before trailing a kiss down her neck.

"Do you think that's wise?" she'd asked breathlessly. His hands had been all over her and her body had been thrumming with pleasure.

"It's just one night. Not a lifetime."

And then he'd kissed her, before scooping her up in his arms and carrying her to bed…

She coughed nervously, trying to dispel the vivid memory. "No, I don't think that's wise."

"Of course it is. You can have my room and I'll be more than comfortable on my large sectional couch. And your cousin will be asleep in the room next to Evan tonight."

Sleeping in a bed was far more ideal than trying to cram herself onto the clinic's couch. Even if that bed belonged to the one man she'd sworn never to go to bed with again. And he'd be far away in the living room on his couch.

"Okay. Thank you."

Chris nodded. "It's the least I can do after you missed your ferry to help me."

"Well, it's my job. I *am* a surgeon too—not just a wrangler of bachelors."

He grinned at her. "True—and you're a damn fine surgeon, if my memory serves me correctly."

She blushed, heat flushing her cheeks as they closed down the clinic.

They began to walk back to his home.

"What about the scooter?" she asked.

"The headlight is burned out, and I really don't feel like riding a scooter after what happened tonight. I'll have to get a helmet before I attempt that scooter again. It's not really proper for a world-renowned neurosurgeon to be terrorizing the streets of Mythelios on a scooter without a helmet."

Naomi laughed at the image of him terrifying people on his scooter and then got an image of her *yia-yia* terrorizing people on a scooter—because she didn't know what Chris's *yia-yia* had looked like, so couldn't picture her, but assumed that she must've been a lot like her own *yia-yia*.

"You're cursed!"

She frowned, shaking her *yia-yia's* voice from her head.

"You okay?" he asked as they ambled up the hill toward his house.

"Yeah, just thinking about my late *yia-yia*. She wasn't as free-spirited as it sounds like yours was."

Chris chuckled softly. "I don't think many were—and her free spirit caused my father many gray hairs. As do I, truth be told. I have a bastard heir."

Naomi winced. "That sounds like something out of an old Victorian novel. There are a lot of unmarried parents these days. Families are no longer traditional."

"Tell that to my father. Although he never really liked having kids either. It was just what was expected of him. So he and my mother had me, and then my mother grew disenchanted, or bored—I don't know—and she left. Though as far as I know, my parents are still legally married. My father doesn't believe in divorce either."

"I'm sorry."

"And what of *your* family? I didn't know that you were half-Greek."

"Well, we didn't really ever talk about our families when we were together, did we?"

Which was true, as the time they'd spent together they had been either working in the hospital or in bed together. Maybe that was why she'd been so blindsided when Chris had upped and left her for Manhattan.

She'd been so blinded by love that she hadn't been expecting it.

Lust, not love. Remember that.

And that was what she had to keep telling herself. As she'd picked up the pieces of her heart, she'd come to realize that it hadn't been love, and that their whole relationship had been built on lust. She'd been a fool.

"So tell me about them. You know about mine—or rather the whole world seems to know about mine, since my father is one of the wealthiest men in the Aegean."

"My father was Greek, but he left Athens and went to America when he was a very young man. He met my mother in Nashville, they fell in love and here I am. My father brought me only once to Greece when I was a young girl, when I met his mother and a few of my other Greek relatives. But it didn't go all that smoothly, thanks to *Yia-yia*, and we never came back. Or at least *he* didn't come back. He passed away last year. When I saw a posting in Greece to help with the earthquake relief, I thought I'd return."

"I'm sorry to hear of your father's passing," Chris said gently, his voice somber.

"Thank you. I loved my father. We were very close— particularly after my mom died a few years ago."

"And your Greek family? Lisa is your cousin?"

Naomi smiled. "Yes. I'm glad we're getting to know each other now. All my older cousins are boys, and when I came here, I was only about fourteen, so we didn't really have that much in common."

Chris chuckled. "No, I suppose you wouldn't."

"Do *you* have a large family?" she asked.

"No. Just my parents. My father was an only child and I'm an only child. If there are cousins on my mother's side, I don't know them. My mother left my father and me when I was quite young. She's in Corfu now. I have reached out to her over the years, but she wants nothing to do with me. I remind her of all the things she never wanted."

"I'm sorry... Did she actually *say* that to you?" Naomi asked, horrified.

He nodded. "Yes. Marrying my father was her parents' idea, and marrying him and having a child ended her medical career. So even though I became a surgeon—a world-renowned one at that—she sees it as a final betrayal. I became what she never could."

"That's really very selfish of her."

Chris chuckled again. "Yes, well, I won't deny that my parents are selfish—or that I was."

His admission of selfishness caught her off guard. She'd never thought she'd hear that coming from him. Perhaps he'd matured and grown now he was a father. Maybe he'd really changed.

Don't fall for the same trap again, Naomi.

They walked in silence the rest of the way. He unlocked the door and led her up the stairs of his late grandmother's house, which was still laid out in the traditional way of all the old houses that littered the islands of Greece and the mainland.

She laid her hand on the stone, which was cool. There was a large, modern-style kitchen at the top of the stairs. He led her out through the kitchen into a small covered courtyard that held a small table, and she heard the bubbling sounds of water from a small fountain in the middle of the courtyard.

He pointed through another set of French doors. "That's the living room, and there are stairs there that lead to Lisa's room and Evangelos's room. My room is this way."

Chris led her upstairs, higher up the cliff that this winding house had been built into. There was a solid balcony, and from there Chris took her straight into his room.

"This is a beautiful house," she said, suddenly feeling awkward as she eyed the large bed that dominated the room.

Chris nodded. "It needs some work. The bathroom is through that door, and there's another small courtyard off the bathroom, and then stairs down to the garden, where there's a small pool. From the courtyard there are more stairs down to the hallway that connects Lisa's and Evan's rooms."

"It's a maze!"

He smiled. "A bit—but this house has been in my *yia-yia's* family for a long time. They built it slowly. It does need some updating—like putting in air-conditioning— but if you leave the balcony doors open, and these windows too, you'll get a nice cross breeze this high up."

"Thank you again. I hate that I'm depriving you of your bed tonight."

"It's no bother, really. My living room is quite comfortable. Let me just grab a couple of things and I'll leave you to it."

Chris gathered some things and then headed for the balcony door, where he paused and turned around. "If you need anything, please let me know."

"I will. Thank you."

He nodded and left.

Naomi could see out of windows that faced down into the courtyard, and saw when he crossed it and headed into the living room. He closed the French doors to the living room and then the house was quiet.

She headed over to the other side of the room and

opened the windows, sighing when she saw the sea and the bright moon reflected over the diamond-dappled waters. Her place in Athens didn't overlook the sea, but there was quite a nice view of the Parthenon…

She cleaned up in the bathroom and changed out of her work clothes. She wrapped one of the cotton sheets around her to sleep and settled down in the bed.

It was comfortable and it smelled like Chris. A scent she'd never forget because she often thought of being wrapped up in his arms.

He'd changed.

You don't know that.

She sighed, ignoring that niggling thought. She needed to get a good night's rest. There was a lot to do tomorrow and she planned to be up and out of here before Chris got up.

She couldn't get involved with him again. She'd promised herself that she'd keep her distance from him, but that was hard to do when she was staying in his house and sleeping in his bed.

She'd be gone before he got up and tomorrow they'd continue working together. Friendly, but that was it. That was as far as it could go.

She had to keep reminding herself of that or she'd fall into the same trap again.

A trap that would cost her her heart—and she couldn't afford to let it be broken again.

CHAPTER FIVE

WARM SUNLIGHT STREAMING through the window was
what woke her up. She was disoriented, and her eyes
were having a hard time adjusting to the bright light
that was filtering in from the windows.

This was not her small apartment in Athens and,
judging by the sounds filtering in through the open windows, it was past time that she usually got up.

Oh, no. I slept in.

Naomi groaned and glanced at the small clock next
to the bed and saw that it was actually nine-thirty in
the morning.

Great.

So much for her plan to slip out of the house early
and avoid Chris. She got up and pulled on her clothes
from the night before, cleaned herself up and made her
way out to the balcony and down through the courtyard
into the kitchen.

Chris was sitting at the large wooden table and in a
high chair next to him was Evangelos. Chris was feeding the baby yogurt and the baby's face lit up as he eagerly opened his mouth and gulped down the yogurt
while banging his little fists against the plastic table of
the high chair.

She couldn't help but smile at the sight. The baby

was covered in yogurt and making little noises of pleasure as Chris fed him.

It sent a pang of longing through her, which caught her off guard. She had to get a hold of herself. She couldn't be thinking this way. She couldn't feel the pain right now and she had to keep her walls intact. That was the only way her heart would survive working with Dr. Moustakas again.

The alternative—crumbling before him and letting him see the vulnerable side to her...the side that was still mourning what she'd lost—was not an option.

"Good morning," she said, feeling completely awkward as she stepped into the kitchen and interrupted this moment between Chris and his son.

"Good morning," he said, glancing briefly over his shoulder. "You slept in. I half expected you to be gone when I got up, but Lisa checked on you before she left for the market and said you were still sound asleep."

"I'm afraid I didn't hear the alarm I set for myself."

"Ah, yeah—that clock doesn't work beyond telling the time. I usually just use my phone. Sorry, I should have told you."

"It's no problem."

"There's coffee," he said, and he got up and poured her a cup, holding it out to her.

"Thank you."

She took a sip and it hit the spot. She sat down across the table from him and his son. The baby grinned at her and then gurgled, demanding more yogurt.

"Yes, yes. So impatient." Chris beamed and spooned the last of the yogurt into the baby's mouth.

Naomi smiled. "He's adorable."

"I think so," Chris said, with pride in his voice. "Oh,

Lisa left a pair of shoes in her room for you. Some ballet flats until you can get back to Athens."

"Good to know," Naomi said, relieved. "I wasn't sure how it would look, wearing flip-flops in the clinic two days in a row."

Chris chuckled. "It's not safe, that's for sure."

"Have you had any updates on Maximos?" she asked.

"Yes, as a matter of fact I have…"

Chris cleaned up Evangelos and handed the baby a toy to play with as he put the yogurt dish in the sink.

"The hospital in Athens was able to stabilize him, but he needs surgery, and their surgeons have never dealt with a depressed skull fracture of this magnitude. They want me to go and perform the surgery this evening. So I'll be heading to Athens tonight and then coming back to Mythelios in the morning."

"I'm sorry to hear that Maximos's condition is so severe. His poor mother must be beside herself."

Chris nodded. "It's hard to be so hurt and so far from home, even if Athens isn't technically that far away. I hope I can do something, but I won't know until I get in there."

"What about Evangelos?" She glanced at the baby, who was already drifting off to sleep in his high chair. His chubby cheeks were even more pronounced as he slept.

"Lisa will watch him. He'll be in good hands and I'll be back in the morning." Chris set down his coffee. "I'll just put him down, and then once Lisa gets back, we can walk to the clinic together."

"Sure."

She drank her coffee slowly as Chris picked up Evangelos, who was startled but then curled into his father's arms. It made her long once again for the baby she'd lost, and she choked back the emotion that was welling up in her.

She just couldn't help but wonder *what if?*—which was something she never let herself do. She didn't ever let herself think about what had been lost, because it had taken her so long to pull the pieces of her heart back together.

"I'm back," Lisa called out as she came up the stairs. "Good morning, sleepyhead."

"Hey—so you have shoes I can borrow?"

Lisa nodded and set the bags from the market on the table. "Yes. Come to my room and you can try them on, but I'm pretty sure they'll fit you."

Naomi set her coffee cup in the sink and followed Lisa through the courtyard and into the living room. She could see sheets at one end of the large sectional couch where Chris had obviously slept.

Warmth spread in her cheeks as she thought of him stretched out there, sleeping...

She had rolled over and looked at him. He'd been sleeping on his back, with one arm behind his head and one resting across his chest. Only a sheet had covered his hips. She'd watched him breathing in deep sleep, recalling the way his arms had held her after their lovemaking. How safe she'd felt with him.

She'd reached out and touched his chest, running her fingers over his skin.

He'd opened an eye and smiled at her.

"Good morning..."

She had to focus.

She couldn't let memories like that invade her thoughts. She had to lock all those memories away, and not *feel* when it came to Chris, so that she could protect her heart.

Up a few more steps and they were in Lisa's small but comfortable room. Lisa picked up a pair of black flats from her bed and held them out.

"These should fit you."

Naomi sat on the edge of Lisa's bed and slipped the shoes on. They were a little big, but not much.

"These are perfect. I'll bring them back to you tomorrow."

"No rush. Now, I'd better go check on Evangelos so Chris can get back to work. He's heading to Athens tonight?"

Naomi nodded. "Maximos Ponao was in an accident last night and he has a pretty significant skull fracture."

Lisa sighed. "He was one of those good-looking men from the market who were watching us the other day. That's too bad."

"He was?"

"Don't you remember? You don't see any of the men who have eyes for you, Naomi," Lisa teased as she slipped out of the room.

She hadn't given those two handsome Greek gods any thought after that day in the market when she'd had lunch with Lisa because all she could think about was Chris. When Chris was around, she didn't see any other man.

She hadn't dated after Chris and her miscarriage because even the thought of being intimate with another man made her remember what she'd lost, and she didn't ever want to be hurt like that again. It was better to focus on her work, so that she could forget the pain.

But here she couldn't hide from it.

And she hated that.

She hated the feeling that she was losing control of

herself, because she'd sworn that she wouldn't make that mistake again.

"Thank you for the shoes. I'm going to head back to the clinic. Tell Chris thank you for letting me crash here for the night."

"Sure thing."

Naomi left the room, and as she glanced back into Evangelos's room, she saw Chris rocking back and forth, the baby over his shoulder.

Tears stung her eyes.

She had to get out of here before she did something she'd regret.

Naomi was avoiding him and he didn't know why.

Lisa had come in to take over the care of Evan so that he could get to the clinic, and when he'd gone to pack a bag for his overnight stay in Athens, he'd discovered that Naomi had left and gone to the clinic without him.

He'd foolishly thought that they might walk down together. He'd thought they'd gotten past the awkward stage and were becoming friends again, because that was all he really wanted.

Liar. You want a lot more than to be her friend.

He cursed himself inwardly and rubbed his eyes as he leaned back in his office chair. He was staring at the scans that the Athens hospital had sent over so he could prepare for the surgery on Maximos.

He hadn't practiced surgery since Evangelos had been born. His life had been in complete upheaval since then. Evan had been born, he'd had to pay off Evan's birth mother, Lillian, from the funds he'd had to beg from his father and then the earthquake had happened. And finally his *yia-yia* had become sick and died.

He was looking forward to getting back into the operating room, even if the team in Athens wasn't his usual team. Maximos needed surgery and he had the skill and experience to do it.

And, deep down, he was really looking forward to not being a father tonight—so he had to stop thinking about Naomi and how she was avoiding him and focus on work.

He had no time in his life for a relationship, and he would never bring a woman into his life unless he was committed to her completely. He didn't want to hurt Evan that way. He didn't want his son to feel like *he'd* felt growing up. Evan had already been abandoned by one mother, and that was one too many as far as Chris was concerned.

Focus.

He leaned over the computer again and made some notes. He could definitely use more coffee. He hadn't gotten much sleep last night. Evan had mostly slept, but the couch was not Chris's bed and he hadn't been able to stop thinking about who was in it.

She'd been so close, but so far out of his reach.

And he hadn't been able to stop thinking about all those nights they had spent together. Her in his arms, the silky feather-like touch of her hair against his cheek, the scent of jasmine and how she'd driven him wild...

If only it had been *her* who had gotten pregnant with his child. *She* would've never left their baby.

Or at least he'd like to think that. He didn't really know her, did he?

He glanced at his watch and saw that the ferry was going to leave soon. He finished making his notes and grabbed his stuff out of the staff lounge.

"Off to Athens?" Theo asked as he came out of an exam room.

"Yes. The surgery is tonight. Is Dr. Hudson still here?"

"No, she left for the ferry a few moments ago. Why?"

Chris frowned. "No reason. I left Lisa your number in case something happens with Evan…"

"No worries. She'll have it handled, I'm sure."

Chris nodded. He'd been apart from Evangelos for several hours before, but usually he stayed within a ten-mile radius of his son. This was the first time that sea would be separating them, so he couldn't get to him quickly.

It was scary, but as a parent he should think about *his* son being the one on the operating table, dependent on the surgical skills of a particular doctor. He would want the very best for Evan, so he had to do this for someone else's son.

"I'm sure too," Chris said quickly. "I'll see you all tomorrow."

He left the clinic and headed down to the docks. The ferry was boarding, and he handed in his ticket and went on board to the upper deck. As he got there, the ferry made its final preparations and was soon pulling away from Mythelios and toward the mainland.

He took a deep breath and leaned against the railing, watching the island slip into the distance, all the while trying not to worry about his baby too much. When he could no longer see the island, he turned back away from the railing—and saw that Naomi had taken a seat inside. She was reading papers from a very thick file.

Just let her be. She doesn't want to be with you.

Only, he couldn't take his own advice and he made his way to her.

"You didn't wait for me."

Naomi looked up, startled. "Chris! No, I guess I didn't. You were so absorbed with those scans from

Athens that I thought I'd sneak down to the ferry and start doing my work."

"No, I mean this morning. You didn't wait for me then either," he said, taking a seat next to her.

"I have a lot of work to do."

"I thought you were running away."

A strange expression crossed her face briefly. "And what would I be running from?"

"Me?"

"I did that already," she stated firmly, and then turned back to her work.

"Would you be in the operating room with me?"

The words stunned him, but he really needed someone he trusted in that room when he worked on Maximos. If he couldn't have his regular scrub nurse and the residents he was used to working with, he could at least have *her*.

They worked very well together. And she had been there from the start with Maximos.

She was clearly shocked. "You want *me* to be in the operating room with you?"

"You're still a neurosurgeon. Who else would I have in there with me? I don't know many of the surgeons in Athens. I haven't had a chance to get to know them. I need someone I trust. Besides, I let you sleep in my bed last night. You owe me."

She smiled at him then. "Of course I'll assist you in the surgery. I would like to see the end of that case."

Chris sat back in his chair, more at ease. "Good. I'm glad. I want us to be friends, Naomi. I know things didn't end well for us, but I want us to be friends and colleagues."

A blush bloomed in her cheeks. "I would like that too."

"Good." He leaned over and glanced at her paperwork. "Is this about the bachelor auction?"

"Yes. We have a lot of interesting bachelors. A famous Greek singer and an actor."

She held out the list and he was impressed with the names.

"We should be able to raise enough money to donate to the Mythelios Free Clinic and continue helping with the relief efforts elsewhere too."

"That's good. The earthquake was devastating on so many levels. It nearly decimated the infrastructure of Mythelios. Not only were so many injured, but the water supply was compromised and the island was without power for days. And without clean water, disease and dehydration caused a lot of the medical emergencies."

Naomi nodded. "I know. Ever since I started working with this organization, I've seen and helped with so many disasters. I've just never had this kind of public relations nightmare shoved on me with such short notice before. I'd prefer to be helping the wounded and the sick—not doing all this fund-raising stuff. It's frustrating, but I know it's necessary, and so here I am, doing it."

"Well, put it away for now and focus on the surgery at hand. What do you know about a comminuted skull fracture affecting the parietal, sphenoid and frontal bone? As well as a depressed skull fracture of the temporal bone."

"The patient is suffering from all that?" Naomi was shocked, as a comminuted skull fracture meant that the skull had been broken into three sections. He was lucky to be alive after so much trauma to his head.

Chris nodded. "We didn't see it last night, with all the swelling, but now we have that managed there's more, and they've emailed across updated scans so I can see the work ahead of us. It will probably be a long night."

"That's okay. I want to help. I feel sorry for such a handsome young man."

Chris cocked an eyebrow. "You had time to notice if he was handsome or not?"

"No." Pink bloomed in her cheeks. "It's not that. When I was out to lunch with Lisa, she mentioned that there were two handsome young men checking us out, and she reminded me this morning that the patient was one of them. If he was, those two men were both quite striking and, yes, young."

A surge of jealousy flared in him and he was surprised by it because he had no right to feel that way. Why shouldn't Naomi date someone else? He had no claim on her. He was the one who broke it off. He was the one who had passed her over for his career.

"Well, we'll see what we can do for him," he managed to say.

"Any word about Stavros?" she asked, breaking the tension that had settled between them.

"No, he hasn't come back to me. I do hope he gives me an answer soon, because I'd like to get started on treatment as soon as possible. With that form of aggressive tumor, the best course is to start treatment quickly, but he hasn't even agreed to a full body scan yet."

"Perhaps he doesn't want to know. If it's worse than he thinks it is already, perhaps his lack of answer is an answer in itself."

"He should fight if he has a chance. He shouldn't give up. *I* wouldn't. Would you?"

"No, I suppose I wouldn't—but if there was no hope, then I wouldn't put myself through painful surgery and chemotherapy. Although I see the point you're trying to make."

After that they sat there quietly, barely talking.

The ferry docked in Athens and they disembarked.

"Do you want to split a cab to the hospital?"

"I have to go to my apartment and grab some comfortable shoes," she said. "Shoes that are suited to the operating room."

He chuckled. "I suppose so. I'll meet you in the scrub room, then."

She nodded.

Chris opened the cab door and she climbed in. It sped off through the busy streets of Athens—or rather Piraeus, as that was where the docks were. He sighed, thinking about the task at hand and hoping that he could live up to the reputation he'd thought he'd left behind in Manhattan.

CHAPTER SIX

HIS PULSE WAS racing as he stood in the scrub room, watching through the window as the surgical team prepped the room and the patient. He hadn't started scrubbing in yet, but he had on his scrub cap.

You got this.

He didn't know what he was waiting for. Perhaps he was waiting for a sign.

He took a deep breath and used his foot to turn on the water, which was soon warm, and he started scrubbing with the soap. He hadn't done any surgery in over eight months. It felt good to be back, but he wasn't sure he completely deserved it.

"Just in the nick of time," Naomi said as she came into the room.

Her strawberry blond hair was braided and done up in a bun under her scrub cap. Just like she'd always had it before. And the familiar sight set his nerves at ease.

She was so good. Too good for him.

"I thought you weren't going to make it in time. I thought I'd have to do this on my own," he teased.

"Never. You are the best in the world at neurosurgery. I couldn't miss out on working with you again. Just like old times."

"Some of the best times, I hope. But I'm not a god."

"Tell that to the hospital in Manhattan," she teased. "In all seriousness, Chris, I wouldn't let you down. Maximos is my patient too."

He smiled and nodded, continuing to scrub. She never had let him down. Yet he'd let *her* down.

I don't deserve her.

"I want to do a craniotomy. Last scan shows an aneurysm, and I want to get in there and clip it before I even begin to think of how to tackle the rest of his head injuries," he said, shaking that thought out of his mind.

"He's going to need a long recovery."

Chris nodded. "It will be painful. It will really hurt when he wakes up. I don't envy him. I hope that he's a fighter."

"Look how long he's held on," Naomi remarked. "He's a fighter, I'm sure."

Chris wanted to hold on to that thought. He needed to hold on to that shred of hope so that it would wash away his nerves.

You got this.

He dried his hands, pulled up his mask and stepped through the door into the sterile environment of the operating room. The scrub nurse met him and helped him into the surgical gown and gloves. He bent down so the nurse could put on his headlight and glasses.

He rolled his shoulders to ease the mounting tension and approached the head of the table. He looked up and saw that he was operating in a room with a gallery that was packed with other physicians. All watching.

It caused his pulse to kick up a notch.

"What's going on?" he asked.

"Sorry, Dr. Moustakas. The chief of surgery would like his residents and interns to observe your surgery.

You're a bit of a legend and you're in our hospital," the scrub nurse said nervously.

Just what he didn't want.

Before Evangelos, when he'd been living his life at full speed without a seat belt, he would have welcomed this. He would have eaten up the adoration. But now he felt he didn't deserve the accolades. That this was all too much.

You got this.

The operating room door opened and Naomi walked in. He let out a sigh of relief on a breath that he hadn't known he was holding as she was gloved, gowned, and then joined him at the head of the table.

"You okay?" she asked as she stood next to him.

"Perfectly. Why?"

"You seem nervous—or maybe it's just the atmosphere in the room. You have quite the audience."

"Don't remind me," he grumbled.

He closed his eyes and held out his hand.

"Scalpel."

The nurse placed the instrument in his hand and he made the first incision—and with that first cut everything came rushing back to him. All he thought about was what he was doing. Everything else faded into the background. All his fears of forgetting what he was doing disappeared, and in his mind he could see the correct way forward, what he'd done countless times before.

And working beside him, anticipating his every move, was Naomi. She knew what to do before he had to tell her. It was as if they were one surgeon, instead of two, and it made the hours of surgery fly by in an instant.

Before he knew it, they were finishing up and the

patient was being closed by the resident who had been chosen to work with them.

The students in the gallery were applauding politely as he walked away from the patient to the scrub room, and it was then that the many hours of being in surgery after months of being out of practice finally hit him. He felt as if his body weighed a ton and his eyes were lined with sandpaper.

He leaned against the wall after he'd peeled off his surgical gown, gloves and mask. Then he made his way to the sink to scrub out.

Naomi joined him. "You were brilliant," she said, smiling.

Her eyes were bright and warm, making him feel he was actually wanted.

"Thank you. You were too, by the way. I don't think I would've handled it as well without you."

She blushed. "Thank you."

He loved the way she blushed. The pink in her cheeks made him think about kissing her over and over. He cleared his throat to shake the sudden inappropriate thoughts out of his mind.

"What time is it? Any chance I could catch the ferry back to Mythelios?" he asked.

"I hate to tell you, but no. You've worked all night and it's now almost noon. That was a whopper of a surgery—which took even longer because you had to clamp that aneurysm."

He swore under his breath. "I'll have to call Lisa and tell her that I won't be home until the evening ferry now. At least the hospital has on-call rooms where I can rest for a couple of hours."

"That it does—and you *should* rest," she said. "I

would offer you my bed, and repay the debt, but I live in a tiny stamp-sized apartment that's only one room."

His blood heated at the thought of having to share a small apartment with her.

Focus.

"Thank you for the offer, but I told you the debt was repaid by you assisting me on this surgery. I truly appreciate it."

"Anytime. Would you like to get something to eat after you've rested? Do your postoperative notes, catch forty winks and then come and have some lunch with me in Athens? Remember we always used to have a postsurgical celebratory dinner?"

He grinned. "And that was always followed by something else. Something more pleasant."

What are you doing?

Only, he couldn't help but flirt with her.

She blushed again. "It would only be dinner this time—in fact, it would actually be a late lunch as you need to catch the last ferry back, remember?"

"Of course. Yes, sure—I *would* like that. I have to eat, don't I?"

He was slightly disappointed that it wouldn't lead to something else, but he was mad at himself for even thinking that way about her. For wanting more when he knew perfectly well that if he had her once they would both want more—and he still couldn't give her that.

All he had left to give her was friendship.

"I better go do my postoperative notes and get my head down for a bit. Shall I meet you in the lobby of the hospital at about two?" he asked.

"That sounds good. We can have a leisurely lunch and maybe do a bit of sightseeing before you head back down to Piraeus to make the last ferry home."

She left the scrub room and he leaned against the sink, dropping his head to stare at the drain.

He knew he shouldn't go out to lunch with her, but he was a sucker for punishment. And when it came to her, he deserved every form of punishment that karma threw his way.

What am I doing? What am I doing?

She'd repeatedly asked herself that question ever since she'd invited Chris to lunch. She'd come back to her apartment to change, and something in her gut was telling her she was a making a huge mistake. She'd been overcome by his request that she assist him in surgery, and then in the operating room she'd gotten to see him in action again.

She'd forgotten how amazing it was to work with him. To have him trust her in his operating room. And she'd forgotten how they truly did work so well together.

She'd been in many operating rooms, both as the lead and the assisting surgeon, but when she was with Chris, it was like magic, and she couldn't quite put her finger on why. For one glorious moment in time she'd forgotten about their past, forgotten that he'd walked away from her, left her with a baby he knew nothing about, and forgotten how she'd suffered alone when she'd lost their child.

What harm could one little lunch do?

So much...

"Sorry I'm late," Chris called out as he crossed the busy lobby of the hospital. "After I woke up, I had to speak to Maximos's mother and it took longer than I planned. Expect the same if she ever sees you."

He grinned at her. His dark eyes were twinkling and

that perfect smile made her melt. What was it about him that made her let down her guard?

"There's nothing wrong with gratitude," she said. "I'd be pleased."

He chuckled. "Well, she might not kiss you as passionately as she did me."

Naomi started laughing. She couldn't help it. "She *kissed* you?"

"It was quite a good kiss—but she's not a single lady." Chris winked. "Where shall we go?"

"There's a lovely *taverna* down on Pritaniou, and then maybe we could take a stroll around the Acropolis and Parthenon. I have yet to see them."

He cocked an eyebrow. "You've never seen them?"

"I've seen them from a distance, but I haven't actually *seen* them. When I was fourteen, I didn't have much of a chance because my grandmother was dying, and since I've been here this time, I've just been so busy…"

"*Everyone* should have a chance to go to the Parthenon and the Acropolis."

"Well, now I can—and *you* can tell me all about them. I'm relying on you for authenticity," she teased.

"That's putting a lot of pressure on me."

"Good," she said pertly, and she took his arm as they walked out into the bright sun of Athens in the afternoon.

The streets around the hospital were buzzing with traffic, but Chris led her through the hustle and bustle, and they managed to find a cab to take them to the part of the city near the Parthenon and the Acropolis.

An open-air *taverna* sat just below the hill. And even though it was sweltering, the *taverna* was in the shade of some olive trees and had a nice cross breeze.

Chris pulled out a chair for her to sit down and he sat next to her.

A waiter came over and greeted them. "*Yassou*, what can I start you with?" he asked.

"Coffee," Chris said.

The waiter looked at her.

"Water, please," she said.

The waiter nodded and left.

"You're having *coffee* in this heat?" she asked incredulously.

"You forget I don't get much sleep at home with an infant. I'm sure there are bags under my eyes."

"Not too many." She grinned.

The waiter returned with their drinks and they ordered a light lunch of fish and salad.

Chris took a sip of his coffee. "That hits the spot," he said, and leaned back. "I hope the heat breaks before next week, when I have to go up on stage in a tuxedo and be bid on."

"Thank you for doing that. The other doctors in the clinic were all going to step up, but…"

"Yeah, they're all conveniently taken," he grumbled, but then he smiled. "I don't mind. Though I don't know what a single father can offer…"

"You have a lot to offer. You're a doctor, and being such a caring father is very attractive to most women."

"Is it?"

"Oh, yes."

"And how about you? Is it attractive to *you*?"

Affection glowed in his eyes and it made her catch her breath. She could feel warmth flooding her cheeks. Before she could answer the question, the waiter returned with their fish and salad.

They continued chatting about the surgery, and mundane things about the clinic and the hospital. When they were finished, and the waiter had taken everything away, he caught her off guard again.

"Are you going to be bidding on anyone at the auction?" he asked.

"What?" she asked, almost choking on her water.

"I asked if you will be bidding. You organized it, but surely you can bid too—and if so what kind of date are you looking for?"

"I don't think we should be talking about this," she said quickly, looking away.

"Why? Are we not friends? You said so yourself."

"Of course we're friends." She sighed. "Okay…no, I will not be bidding on anyone because I will be hosting the event. I'll be doing the auctioning, so I can't really bid on one of the lots, can I?"

"That's disappointing, but I get it."

She opened her purse and paid for her half of the bill. "I have so much on my plate I can't even *think* about dating anyone—even for charity. I'm way too busy."

And that was the way she liked it. Being busy meant she didn't have time to think about the pain, or the way her heart ached when she thought about what might have been.

He tossed down the rest of the amount owed and then pulled out her chair before they left the *taverna* and headed out onto the street, up the hill toward the Parthenon.

"Well, at least the line is short today," Chris said as they took their spot in line to pay for admission. "And this is my treat. You've never been, and I've been way too many times."

"Thank you," she said. "I'm looking forward to it."

"There's not much left of it, but the views of the city are worth the price."

He paid for their tickets and they were ushered through the gate and were soon wandering through stones and crumbling ruins.

As they moved away from the regular tourists, Chris put a hand on the small of her back, and her body came alive with just that simple touch from him.

"See—look at the views over the city. Can you imagine what this must have been like when it was all brand-new?" he said wistfully.

"You mean when Zeus ruled all?" she teased.

A smile quirked at the corner of his lips. "You mean Athena, don't you?"

"That *does* make more sense. Why did they name the city after her?"

"Because she gave its citizens the gift of the olive. It was food, its branches would burn in their hearths and its oil would light their lamps."

"And was there a rival for the citizens' affections?" she asked.

"Poseidon. He struck the ground and gave them a saltwater well—but what could the people do with a saltwater well? They couldn't drink it. Whereas Athena gave them the olive and so Athens was born."

He smiled at her, and that dimple in his cheek made her blood heat, and in that moment, with the loud rush of the city below them and tourists all around them, she saw only him. Heard only him. Drowned everything else out.

Naomi could feel herself melting for him.

Get a grip on yourself.

"Poseidon must've been mad," she said huskily.

"Yes, he caused a flood and drowned a bunch of

people—but I won't say a bad word about the god of the sea…not when I need calm seas tonight to get home to my son."

And he moved away from her then, breaking the spell that had been woven around them.

They finished walking around the Parthenon and the Acropolis and then headed back down the hill, to take a cab to the docks at Piraeus.

"When will you be coming back to Mythelios?" he asked after he'd bought his ticket.

"Tomorrow morning."

He nodded. "I'll pray for calm seas then too."

"I would appreciate it." She tucked a loose strand of hair behind her ear nervously. "I'll check on Maximos tonight. I have a round I need to complete there anyways."

"Thank you. I appreciate it. And I'll feel better leaving him now that I know you'll be there."

The ferry horn sounded and Chris glanced back over his shoulder.

"You'd better go," she said. "You can't leave Evangelos for another night."

"No. I can't." He leaned over and kissed her cheek. "Thank you for helping me with the surgery. It was good having you there beside me again. I'd forgotten what it was like."

"You're welcome. Now, go."

He nodded and walked through the gate toward the ferry.

She sighed and stayed there even though she couldn't see him get on. She watched as the ferry pushed away from port, and continued to watch as it faded into a dot on the horizon, heading off toward Mythelios.

What are you doing?

She wasn't sure what she was doing, to be honest. She was setting herself up for more heartache if she even *thought* about this—but she missed him. Being with him reminded her of how much she'd enjoyed being in his company and how much brighter her life had been in his presence.

But they could be friends and nothing more.

That was the least she could do for her heart.

CHAPTER SEVEN

NAOMI KNOCKED ON the door of one of the exam rooms in the clinic. She'd quickly fallen back into her routine of working at both the clinic and the hospital in Athens. It had been a few days since she'd said goodbye to Chris at the ferry and made that vow to herself that she wasn't going to allow anything to happen between them except friendship.

Friendship she would gladly handle. It would mean a more pleasant work environment.

And so far it had been working well. Although actually she hadn't seen him since they said goodbye in Piraeus, because Evangelos had gotten a bad cold and Chris had been devoting all his time to his son. A baby with a cold wasn't a pleasant thing, and it had taken all her willpower not to run up to his house and check on the both of them.

But she knew she would just be getting in the way if she did that. Lisa was working at his house, and she didn't want to interfere with her cousin's job either.

"Come in."

Naomi opened the door and saw one of her younger patients who'd had his spleen removed a couple of weeks ago was waiting for her.

"How are you feeling today, Giorgos?" she asked.

"Better," Giorgos answered. "But I'll feel fabulous when I can get the all clear. Will that be soon?"

"You ruptured your spleen. You lost an organ. That's not great. You have to recover from major abdominal surgery and your body has to adjust."

Giorgos's mother put her hand on her son. "Dr. Hudson, do we need to pay anything toward the surgery? Giorgos wants to work. He's of age, and his father…"

"I understand, Mrs. Veritas, but he can't work. Not yet. He needs to rest. He's only two weeks post-op from his splenectomy. But the loss of his spleen was as a result of an unstable structure in the aftermath of the earthquake, so whatever the Greek national health care system can't pick up will be paid for by International Relief."

Mrs. Veritas let out a sigh of relief. "Oh, thank goodness. I was trying to work it all out in my head."

"It's okay. It's taken care of. He would've died had he not been flown to Athens and had the spleen removed."

Giorgos didn't look too pleased, but she couldn't blame the boy. He was seventeen, and he wanted to get back to the things that he liked, which included sports. And he'd lost his father in the earthquake. The boy was now head of the household.

Giorgos wanted to work. He wanted to fill his father's shoes. Except losing a major organ was putting a crimp in his plans.

"After we take the stitches out, you will have to go on some medication, which will also be covered by International Relief. I'm sorry, Giorgos, but I think you're on bed-rest for a while yet. Your white count is elevated, which suggests that your body is fighting an infection, and you're not healing as fast as I would like."

"Malakas!" Giorgos cursed.

His mother gasped. "Such language in front of the doctor!" Mrs. Veritas screeched.

"Sorry, Dr. Hudson," Giorgos said contritely. "That earthquake caused more trouble than good."

"Don't they always?" Naomi asked. "But you're alive. If you rest now, then you can help out your family when you're as good as new."

Giorgos frowned anxiously. "When will that be?"

"Six more weeks," Naomi said. "I'll call you in to clear you in six weeks—but that's only if you rest so your body can heal. If you have any issues, like fever, which is a sign of a postoperative infection, come to the clinic right away. Don't worry about the cost."

"Thank you, Dr. Hudson," Mrs. Veritas said, and she and her son left the clinic.

Naomi sighed and made a note in her chart. There was a knock on the door and she looked up to see Chris hovering in the doorway. There were dark circles under his eyes, worse than usual, and she felt bad for him.

"Hey," she said. "How is Evan?"

"Better, thank God. That was *brutal*. He was so congested—and I won't explain to you the horrors of trying to relieve a baby of nasal congestion."

Naomi laughed. "I already know, but thanks for that mental picture."

Chris slipped into the room and shut the door. "I need your help."

"Sure—with a case?"

"No. My father."

"What about your father?" she asked.

"He's coming to visit me tonight."

"Oh?"

Chris nodded. "I need you to come over for dinner. I tried to get Ares, Theo and Deakin to come over with their significant others, but apparently they're all too busy. I don't believe it for one second. They just don't want to see my father. Not that I blame them—I don't want to see my father either."

"So I get that honor instead?" she asked, arching a brow.

"You *have* to help me. If you're there, maybe he'll ease up on me, and we can steer the conversation away from how I wasted my money on the clinic, and how terrible a son I am for not following in his footsteps. Maybe he won't point out so many of my faults if there's a pretty woman dining with us tonight."

"If you think it will help, then sure. Does he know about the upcoming bachelor auction?"

"I hope not—but probably." Chris rolled his eyes. "You're really doing me a solid favor here. I owe you one. He's a bit of a bully. I hope you won't get upset if he acts like a jerk toward you."

"It's no problem—and bullies I can handle. I didn't get where I am in my career by bowing down to pompous, arrogant people."

He smiled, relief washing over his face. "Thank you. So—come to my place around seven. He'll be arriving about eight."

"Sounds good—but I'm warning you already that I'm going to call in my favor later this week."

He cocked an eyebrow. "Oh…?"

She handed him Giorgos's chart. "Splenic rupture. It's a seventeen-year-old boy and I really would like someone else to be familiar with his case should he come in while I'm not here. He was injured when an unstable building that had actually been cleared by engineers came crashing down on him about two weeks ago. He'd been working in construction since his father died in the earthquake back in May."

Chris pulled out a pair of glasses and read the chart she'd handed to him. She was surprised to see him wearing glasses. He'd never worn them before. But they didn't detract from the overall sexy, godlike appeal of him. They enhanced it even more and her heart skipped a beat.

"That's bad. Poor kid." He took off the glasses and slipped them back into the breast pocket of his lab coat. Then he looked at her, realizing she was staring at him. "What?"

"Since when did you start wearing glasses?"

"A year ago. I only need them if I've been staring at a computer screen too long, or when I have to focus hard on small details on things like X-rays. I'm not getting any younger."

"You're aging well. Like a fine wine."

Heat bloomed in her cheeks as she realized she'd let that thought slip from her lips instead of keeping it firmly inside her head, where it belonged.

A strange expression crossed his face and a smile quirked his lips as he crossed his arms. "Is that so…?"

She cleared her throat. "Would you get out of here? *You* have to prepare for your father's arrival and *I* have things to do!"

He ran a hand through his hair, making it stand up on end. "Right. Thanks again."

Chris left the exam room and Naomi let out the breath she hadn't realized she was holding. She was going to have to get better control over herself. He was just a friend. A work colleague. Nothing more.

He couldn't be anything else.

* * *

Why did you ask her over to dinner?

Chris wasn't sure what he was thinking. All he knew was that he'd missed Naomi these last few days. Leaving her behind at the docks in Piraeus had been harder than he'd imagined. Even though he'd known he would see her the next day, that ferry ride home had been lonely.

But then when he'd gotten home, he'd been overwhelmed with a sick child, a sick nanny and the news that his father was going to be paying him a visit shortly.

Maybe the seas had been calm, but Poseidon was punishing him in other ways for talking up Athena.

He smiled to himself at that thought, but just remembering that time in the Parthenon brought the images of that afternoon with her back into sharp focus.

Being so close to her had reminded him of a simpler time in his life. When he'd been happy. But then he'd remembered how much of a fool he'd been and what a mistake he'd made in walking away from her. Not that he'd had any choice in the matter.

Now she wanted to be his friend, and he wanted that too. He wanted her in the operating room beside him, working with him. He'd forgotten how much he relied on her.

"Dr. Moustakas—Stavros is here to see you," a nurse said, coming up the hallway.

"He is? He doesn't have an appointment, does he?"

"No, but he's hoping you'll see him. He had some time…"

"Of course. Send him into a free exam room and I'll be with him momentarily."

The nurse nodded and headed back to the waiting area of the clinic. Chris ducked into the room where the files were kept and grabbed Stavros's notes. By that time Stavros was already in an exam room, waiting for him.

Chris entered the room to see Stavros pacing up and down. "You wanted to see me?" he asked.

"Yes." Stavros held up his hand and it shook. "It's getting worse and I'm forgetting things. I'm concerned."

"Do you want to have the scan now?" Chris asked. "Have you eaten or drunk anything yet today?"

"No, I didn't feel like it. I *would* like to do it now, if that's possible, Dr. Moustakas. I have time today because I've closed the *taverna*… I'm not saying that I'll agree to you cutting open my head, but I would like to know what I'm dealing with."

"That's wise. I'll have a nurse prep you for a CT scan. Do you have someone in the waiting room?"

"Yes, my wife came with me."

"Good, because you might not be feeling too well after the dyes and the stuff we make you drink."

Stavros wrinkled his nose. "I suppose this is all worth it?"

Chris clapped him on the shoulder. "It is, Stavros. I promise you. Once I get a clear picture of everything that's going on, we can decide what the next step should be."

Stavros nodded. "Thank you, Dr. Moustakas."

"I'll send a nurse in."

Chris left the room and sent a nurse to prep Stavros for the CT scan.

It took a couple of hours for the prep and the dyes to take effect, but soon Stavros was lying down on the bed of the CT scanner and Chris was in the other room, watching for the scans to come up.

He put on his glasses and watched as the images came up on the screen. As he went through each image, he could get a better look at the anaplastic oligodendro-glioma that was growing in his temporal lobe, and he was relieved to see that it hadn't spread anywhere else in Stavros's body.

"Are those Stavros' scans?" Naomi asked, leaning over him.

Being this close to her, he could smell her perfume—and it made him think of things he shouldn't.

Focus.

"It is. The cancer hasn't spread. Which is good news. It means he might actually go through with the sur-gery—but just look at this," Chris said, clicking on one of the scans of the man's head. "This is a monster. It's a complicated and aggressive anaplastic oligodendro-glioma."

"It certainly is—and if he doesn't get it out, he'll have a slow, painful death."

Chris nodded. "I know. Hopefully that will further my cause and get him to go to Athens and have it taken care of. Is there any word about the funding?"

Naomi sighed. "They won't cover it. It's not related to the earthquake, and if he can't wait for a place on the national health care list to come up, he'll have to cover what his private medical insurance won't."

"His medical insurance won't even cover the entirety of my fees," Chris stated. "So I guess I'd better do it pro bono, just to make sure."

Naomi smiled warmly at him. "I *knew* you had a good heart."

"The problem is getting the hospital to agree to the rest... It will be an expensive surgery. Hopefully who-ever is assisting me will also offer up *her* services pro bono?"

Naomi made a funny face. "Of course. What a silly man you are."

Chris grinned. "I can be."

"I'll work on the board at the hospital in Athens. We'll get it taken care of. Convince Stavros of that— and also try to convince him it's not charity. I know he's a proud man."

"I'll take care of it," Chris said. "Don't worry."

"So, this dinner tonight... I don't want to presume, but will I be able to crash at your place afterward, since I'll be missing the last ferry back to Athens?"

His pulse kicked up a notch at the thought of her staying another night. He hadn't even thought of that when he'd asked her to dinner.

"Of course. I'm sorry—I forgot."

"When I agreed to it, I forgot too, to be honest. I'm sorry that I won't be able to dress up for your father. All I have is my business stuff."

"That's fine—that's actually the way he prefers things."

"Good." She got up. "I'll leave you to break the news to Stavros and I'll see you tonight."

"I look forward to it."

Naomi left and Chris let out a breath he hadn't even been aware that he was holding. How could he have been so foolish?

It's because you want her to stay overnight.

Of course, his father would have his boat, so maybe he could take Naomi back to Athens. If Chris put him on the spot, his father wouldn't say no. Naomi might not appreciate it, but it would be better for both of them if she didn't stay the night.

Wouldn't it?

CHAPTER EIGHT

THE BELL RANG at seven.

"Don't worry, Lisa, I got it!" Chris called out as he ran down the steps to the front door.

Naomi was waiting on the front step, holding a bottle of ouzo.

She held it up. "I thought this might make things easier."

He took the bottle from her as she came inside and he shut the door. "This is strong stuff. Yeah, it might help if I can get my father to take enough shots, but he grew up drinking this stuff like water."

Naomi laughed. "It's like my grandpa and his bourbon—or moonshine. That stuff is *horrible*. It'll knock you flat on your butt if you get it from the right place."

Chris chuckled. "Well, we'll take it easy—but thank you for this."

"Where's Lisa?" Naomi asked, following him up the stairs to the kitchen.

"She's in her room. Evan is asleep and she's resting. She's still getting over a cold too. She'll bring the baby out later, after dinner. She's had the pleasure of meeting my father before and says she'd rather keep to her room."

Naomi's eyes widened. "Oh, good Lord, what am I in for?"

"Hold on to your hat," Chris teased.

Naomi wandered out to the terrace. "We're dining al fresco tonight?"

"It's cooler out here."

"I'm going to quickly say hello to Lisa."

Chris nodded. "Good idea."

Naomi slipped in through the living room doors and Chris tried to calm the erratic beating of his heart. His father coming over had him on edge, and the idea of Naomi spending another night under his roof wasn't helping. He seemed to be digging this deep hole for himself—and he wasn't sure how he was going to get out of it.

Naomi returned a couple minutes later. "She was sleeping, so I didn't bother her. Can I help you with anything?"

"No, I have dinner mostly taken care of. Would you like a shot of ouzo?"

"Sure—why not? I can hold my moonshine."

He grinned and poured them two shots. He held it up. *"Yamas."*

"Yamas," she replied, and then downed it. "That's strong, all right."

He laughed and took back the shot glass. "I told you."

"So, how did Stavros take the news? Is he going to go through with the surgery?"

"He'll let me know—but he's having increasingly worse symptoms of anaplastic oligodendroglioma and he really doesn't like it. He has all the facts now, and I'll prepare a battle plan on how to take it out without too much damage to the nerves."

"It'll be good to prepare. Speaking of preparing—is there any topic of conversation I should steer clear of when your father is here?"

"You mean like how we dated a few years ago?"

"Did he know about me then?"

"No," he said. "My father and I aren't close, and I didn't ever tell him about the women I was dating. He knows that I was a bit of a playboy—he read the gossip papers that were floating around—and he knows about Evan's mother because I had to go to him to ask for the money."

"The money?" she said blankly.

"The money his mother demanded from me to keep the child. She was going to get rid of my baby unless I paid her a huge sum of money."

The color drained from Naomi's cheeks and a strange, sad expression crossed her face. "That's horrible!"

"What? That I paid her?"

"No, that she blackmailed you. I thought that you never wanted children."

"I didn't," he admitted. "But I wouldn't want to lose one of my children once I knew they existed."

She looked away and then headed out onto the terrace, as if she was upset. He was confused by her behavior and followed her outside.

"Naomi, are you okay?"

"I'm fine," she said, but her voice shook. "I guess I'm just horrified by the greed of some people."

"Then you'll be horrified all over again when you meet my father. He can be pretty greedy too."

The bell rang again.

Speak of the devil.

"You got this," she said. "You're a brilliant surgeon and a good father. It's his problem if he can't see that."

Chris nodded and then touched her hand. It sent a jolt of electricity through him. Just a simple touch of her skin did serious things to him. He was doomed.

"Thanks for being here."

"That's what friends are for."

She smiled at him, but the smile didn't quite reach her eyes. He could still see sadness in their depths.

He would try to find out more about that later, but right now he had to steel himself against his father. Against the constant disapproval and disappointment his father smothered him with.

He ran down the stairs and opened the door. *"Yassou, Pateras,"* he said formally.

"Yassou," his father responded in clipped tones as he stepped inside his childhood home and began scanning the walls, looking for faults. "There's some cracks in the plaster there."

"From the quake. The house is under renovation, *Pateras*. It takes time."

His father made a *tsk*ing noise under his breath. "You should hire men from Athens to deal with it. They'd get it done. Modernize this house and sell it."

"Why would I sell it?" Chris asked disapprovingly.

"You're not seriously going to *stay* here, are you?"

"Why not?"

"And give up your neurosurgery practice in Manhattan?" his father asked in disbelief.

"You never wanted me to be a surgeon," Chris snapped. "Now suddenly you care about whether I'm giving it up or not?"

"Only if you mean to give up a lucrative business just to grub around in that nothing of a…"

His father trailed off and his eyes widened as Naomi came down the stairs. She was a beautiful woman, and his father did have a soft spot for beautiful women.

Of course, once she started exuding her sparky personality, his father wouldn't be as gracious. His father was too old-fashioned to appreciate an outspoken woman.

"*Pateras*, let me introduce you to Dr. Naomi Hudson. She works with International Relief, the aid agency that is helping us after the earthquake."

His father nodded. "It's a pleasure. I am Nikos Moustakas."

"The pleasure is all mine," Naomi said graciously.

"Come up, *Pateras*. I know you have to get back to Athens tonight and dinner is ready."

Chris shot Naomi a look, which made her chuckle a bit under her breath as she led them up the stairs.

His father glanced around the kitchen. "Well, this is more like it. Very modern."

It would be the closest he'd get to a compliment all night from his father.

"Naomi, why don't you and my father head outside and I'll start serving the food?"

"Sure."

Naomi and his father wandered outside. Chris watched his father as he held out a chair for Naomi and sat next to her.

He took a deep breath. He could get through this.

Although it might take a bit more ouzo than the one bottle Naomi had brought.

Naomi could tell that Chris was uncomfortable in his father's presence. She had never seen him like this, and it almost made him seem a bit more human. In fact, she liked this more mature version of Dr. Christos Moustakas much better than the man she'd originally fallen in love with.

The man who had broken her heart.

Be careful.

She did understand why Chris didn't like his father. Nikos Moustakas was cold, and appeared uncaring, but Naomi couldn't help but wonder if there was a caring father buried deep inside him somewhere. Nikos had obviously been hurt when Chris's mother had left him, and he had built up strong walls to keep everyone out—including his son.

Chris and his father were so alike they'd probably always butt heads, and both of them were so stubborn they couldn't see beyond the end of their noses.

"Where is my grandson?" Nikos asked when they'd finished their dessert and were having a drink of wine.

"He's sleeping. He was ill earlier this week," Chris said.

"If the boy is sleeping, then let him sleep. I will see him next time."

"Oh? And when will *that* be?" Chris snapped.

Nikos shot his son a warning look before he turned to her. "So, Dr. Hudson, tell me—what kind of charity events is your relief agency holding to raise money for the earthquake victims?"

"I'm running a bachelor auction, but charity is not my primary focus. I'm a surgeon first and foremost."

Nikos looked slightly horrified and ignored her latter statement as he turned to Chris. "And you have single men here *agreeing* to take part in this auction?"

"*Pateras*, it's not as bad as it sounds. Women bid for a date. That's all. And it's usually something over the top—like a helicopter ride or... Well, I'm planning a night cruise and dinner on one of your yachts, if you'd be kind enough to donate it for a night."

Nikos looked even more horrified by this. "*You're* one of the bachelors?"

"He is," Naomi said, interrupting. "And his date for the auction is definitely generating the most buzz."

"I don't like it," Nikos stated. "Christos, do you think it's *wise* to be doing this when your track record with women hasn't been the best?"

Chris's back stiffened, and she saw him glare through the dim light of the terrace at his father.

"This is just for charity—and I don't date anymore. I have a son to think about now."

"Exactly," Nikos growled. "You have a son to think about. And what would he think about his father *selling* himself, even if it's for charity?"

"I'll pay to rent someone else's yacht, since you disapprove so much."

Nikos rolled his eyes. "And how would *that* look? I'm a shipping magnate and my son has to *hire out* a yacht for a charity event? I don't think so."

"It's an event you don't approve of, but I think it will bring in lots of money and help raise funds for people in need as well as for the clinic. So, yes, if I have to hire a yacht, I will," Chris snapped.

"I will lend you a yacht, Christos. All this fuss for something that I think will bring you nothing but trouble in the end. Need I remind you of—"

Nikos stopped and eyed her.

"I have to be going. Dr. Hudson—it was a pleasure meeting you. Can I escort you home? It is late…"

"My apartment is in Athens and I've missed the last ferry. I'll stay here."

Nikos frowned. "I can take you to Athens in my boat. You don't need to stay here."

Naomi blushed and glanced over at Chris, who was scowling at his father.

"Chris…?"

"Go with him," Chris said curtly.

Naomi felt as if she was stuck between a rock and hard place. She wouldn't mind sleeping in her own bed tonight, but she didn't want to make Chris mad at her for taking off with his father. Both of them were so stubborn. Exactly the same. Why couldn't they see that?

Nikos didn't wait for her on the terrace but headed through the kitchen and down the stairs.

Chris scrubbed a hand over his face. "I'm sorry you had to see that," he said. "My father is…"

"Don't worry. He's not that bad," she said gently. "If you want me to stay, I can."

"No," he said quickly. "It would be foolish of you not to take the ride. Besides, if you refuse, it'll just make matters worse and then he'll start shouting. Everyone does what he says."

"Except you?"

That made him smile. "I suppose so. Which is why he doesn't like me very much."

"I think you're wrong about that."

Chris snorted in disbelief. "Go. Don't keep him waiting. I'll see you tomorrow."

Without thinking, she leaned over and kissed him on the cheek. "Good night."

His eyebrows arched in surprise and she blushed.

She didn't stick around to gauge his response further or discuss what had happened. Suddenly she was glad she was going to be riding back to Athens with Chris's father.

It would be a good thing to get some distance from Chris right now. She had to remember he was just a friend. A work colleague and nothing more.

There was a luxury sedan with a driver waiting outside, and Nikos opened the door for her. He was quite charming, like his son. The only difference was that he was cold, whereas Chris was warm, but they both kept people at a distance in their own way.

Nikos climbed in beside her and the driver drove away as Nikos pulled the door closed.

"I'm sorry for my son's behavior. He really doesn't think sometimes."

"I think he *does* think. He's very careful about his decisions in the operating room, which is why he's one of the best neurosurgeons in the world."

Nikos grunted in response. "If he's one of the best, why is he here, instead of back in America? And he piddled away good money on that clinic."

"'That clinic' saved so many lives when the earthquake happened, Mr. Moustakas."

"Nikos, please."

"Nikos, then," Naomi said gently. "Your son is a good man, and in my opinion you two are very much alike."

"We are *not*! I would never have had a string of affairs just because my heart was broken over some woman. He gave up a good woman, from my understanding. Ah, well, he's paid the price for *that* mistake."

Nikos turned away and was quiet.

Naomi was stunned.

He'd had all those affairs after he left her because he regretted his mistake in giving her up? It seemed unlikely, and she didn't know how to process the information. If it was true, then karma certainly was biting Chris in the butt.

Still, she thought Nikos was being too hard on his son. Chris was doing right by both baby Evan *and* the clinic. Deep down, regardless of all the mistakes Chris had made, he had a good heart. She could see that. He'd changed.

Still, there was a part of her that was still deeply hurt. That remembered all too vividly how he'd thrown her over for a job. How he'd told her that he never wanted to settle down and have a family.

He'd been so sure, and she was having a hard time trusting him again—trusting that he'd really changed when there were still glimpses of his old self simmering just below the surface. She really didn't want to get hurt by him again.

But then there was that other part of herself. The old part of herself, of who she'd been when she'd first met Chris—the part of her that had believed in love and happily-ever-after and wanted to try again.

They pulled up at the docks and Nikos helped her out of the sedan like a gentleman. They boarded the yacht and the captain waited for instructions.

Nikos turned to her. "I have some business to attend to, but please make yourself at home, Dr. Hudson. I have to arrange a yacht for my son to wine and dine some woman with apparently more money than sense."

"International Relief really appreciates that you're donating the use of one of your yachts for this. The money will help so many that were affected by the earthquake."

Nikos softened. "You're welcome. When we dock, my chauffeur in Athens will take you back to your apartment."

"You're too kind…"

Nikos nodded and disappeared below decks.

Naomi stayed outside. The night air was cool and the sea was calm and there were so many stars glittering in the sky. It was a perfect night.

Too bad she was alone—but that was her choice. It was for the best.

As the yacht pulled away from Mythelios and the island grew smaller, she began to long for something different. For a second chance and a life there with Chris. But Chris had just come here to say goodbye to his grandmother and deal with her affairs after she'd passed. His time on the island might not be permanent.

Chris would most likely return to Manhattan, or even go on somewhere else. And she had a great job and didn't want to give it up to follow a man who probably didn't really want her—not after what had happened between them before.

Even if his father *had* said Chris's string of affairs had been an attempt to get over losing her...

She needed to hear those words from Chris, and he hadn't been very forthcoming about it. She wasn't sure that she could put her whole life on the line again. She'd be a fool if she did—but that old part of her wanted her to take a chance, nonetheless.

"You're cursed, Naomi. Cursed."

She shook her crazy *yia-yia's* words from her head. She had to stop thinking about this. There was so much to do this week. The bachelor auction was coming up fast, and she'd promised to help Chris with Stavros's surgery. Then there was Giorgos, who still needed careful monitoring, and Chris had agreed to help her with that.

She had to focus on her career. That was all she had time for. Because the alternative—love, happiness—had brought about a world of hurt the last time she'd experienced it, and she wasn't willing to put herself through that kind of pain again.

CHAPTER NINE

CHRIS WAS UNUSUALLY quiet the next morning, when they met at the clinic to do an emergency surgery on a patient who was having a gallbladder attack. Not that Naomi could blame him. Things had not gone well with his father the night before.

This was the Chris she remembered from when things had ended between them in Nashville, just before he'd left for Manhattan and hadn't looked back. This quiet, brooding, cold man who had broken her heart. The man she'd almost thrown it all away for.

Although according to Nikos Moustakas, Chris had looked back and regretted it...

Still, Chris hadn't ever said the words, and she wasn't going to pursue it. What was the point? It was ancient history now.

They stood in the small scrub room side by side as their patient was taken away to the post-anesthesia care unit.

"You did good in there," Chris remarked. "I haven't seen a gallstone that big in so long—although, granted, it's been a while since I've assisted in a cholecystectomy. I'm not usually called on to assist a general surgeon."

"Thank you," she said. "I'm glad I was able to help. It just sucks that the patient was so close to rupture. She'd probably been feeling ill for months. She said something about how she thought it was due to the untreated water she'd been drinking after the earthquake. She thought that was making her sick."

"The earthquake did damage the water pipes here, and Mythelios didn't have clean treated water for some time."

"Terrible—what a tragedy. We take things for granted, thinking we'll always have them, until they're gone," she said. "Still, it could have been a lot worse. Her gallbladder could've ruptured, or she could've got pancreatitis—both deadly. At least your clinic was here to help."

Chris didn't say anything. He just continued to brood. She knew he was thinking of how his father felt about the clinic.

"Don't let your father get into your head. Investing in this clinic was the right thing to do. It has saved lives. Many more people would've been lost if it hadn't been here."

"I know that," he snapped. "My father is such a pain in my ass. He doesn't see the value in anything unless it makes him money. He married my mother because she came from a wealthy family. I doubt he loved her."

"I don't know about that," Naomi said, and then she was embarrassed that she'd let that slip.

She didn't want to get involved in his life again, but, inexorably, she was. She was being drawn in slowly but surely, and she had to put a stop to it.

"What're you talking about?"

"I think he may have loved her in the only way he knew how, and maybe he was hurt because she didn't love him back. You said so yourself—your mother left and now she lives in Corfu and wants nothing to do with either of you."

Chris nodded. "That is true."

"You two are so alike. So stubborn."

He shot her a look that was meant to convey the fact that she was crazy. "Well, whatever... But I do not regret opening this clinic with my friends. I care about this island. The only happy parts of my life growing up were spent here with my *yia-yia*."

Chris spoke with such tenderness about his late grandmother. It warmed her heart. But she knew how hard his relationship with his father was. She didn't have that kind of relationship with her parents, so she didn't know what it was like not to have a parent's love.

She felt bad for putting him on the spot and forcing him to take part in the bachelor auction, but it was mostly arranged now and the tickets were sold out. There was a lot of money for charity on the line.

She couldn't get out of it, but she could give Chris a way out.

"Look, if you want to bow out of the bachelor auction, that's fine with me. I kind of pressured you into it and I know you're not comfortable with it. And you weren't happy asking your father for the use of one of his yachts. If you want out of it, I'm okay with that. I don't want your father to have something else to hold over you."

Chris grinned at her and that brooding tension melted away. "No, it's okay. I want to do it—even if it's just to annoy him. Besides, it's to help with relief efforts. It will be fun. I just need a tuxedo. I didn't bring one with me."

"Do you need help picking one out?"

He cocked an eyebrow as he finished scrubbing. "Are you offering to help?"

"Sure—why not? When do you want to get it?"

"I'm going across to Athens tonight, with Lisa and

Evan. Other than Stavros—who has still not decided whether or not to have surgery—I've tied up all my other patients here for the next few days because of the auction. And it will give me a chance to check in on Maximos if I'm in Athens."

"Why are you going over tonight?" she asked.

"Lisa needs a couple of days off before the bachelor auction and her family is in Athens. Anyway, I have to head back now, to pack. Evangelos has a lot of gear."

"I can help, if you like."

"Sure," Chris said. "Only if you want to, though."

"I *do* want to. I'm the one uprooting Evangelos from his home while his father takes part in a bachelor auction."

He chuckled. "He won't even know."

"Babies know more than people give them credit for. You told me before that he's eight months old?"

They walked out of the scrub room and headed toward the small lounge.

"Yes. He was a winter baby. A bit of a New Year's surprise." He scrubbed his hand over his face. "I know you know about how I paid for him…"

"You don't need to explain. You didn't want to lose your child. I know how that—" She stopped herself. "I bet it was a horrible feeling. The thought that someone so awful would take away his life."

"She wasn't *completely* awful, and I like to believe that she wouldn't have done it in the end."

"Does she have any contact with Evan?"

"I offered, but she wouldn't even look at him." Chris sighed sadly. "It was probably easier for her that way. Less painful."

And suddenly Naomi felt sorry for Evan's mother. She didn't want him, but losing a child that you'd carried, even if only for a short time, was devastating. It left a mark on your soul—one that *she* still carried.

They didn't say any more about it and had soon changed into their street clothes and headed back up to his house.

Lisa was busy readying things in the kitchen.

"Where's Evan?" Chris asked as he came up the stairs.

"Sleeping," Lisa responded, holding up the monitor. She set it down again. "I think I have everything I need for him. But I still need to pack for myself. How long are we going to be in Athens again?"

"Five days, I think," Chris said.

"Okay. I'll pack for that."

Lisa came over to Naomi and gave her a kiss on the cheek, then scurried off to her room.

"This is a *lot* of gear," Naomi said as she looked at the meticulously packed bags and the large suitcase.

"Babies are high-maintenance," Chris teased as he did a double-check and threw in a couple more things. "I have to make up some bottles for the trip, and make sure there are enough diapers. Nothing like a stinky diaper on a ferry to make everyone feel seasick."

Naomi laughed. "I'll go check on Lisa."

Chris nodded. "Sure. We'll make it to the ferry on time. I swear."

Naomi headed up to her cousin's room and pulled out the pair of shoes her cousin had lent her a few days ago. "I'm returning these."

Lisa smiled. "Thank you. I'll pack them. You could've left them in Athens, I suppose."

"I didn't know exactly when you were coming," Naomi said. "Do you need any help?"

"No, I think I know what I'm packing. I'm going to

be staying with my parents for a couple of days, and I have a lot of plans with friends while I'm there. You should come out clubbing with us."

"I'm past the days of going to clubs, I'm afraid," Naomi said with a rueful smile. Just the idea of clubbing it with her younger cousin made her cringe.

"Well, you *do* have to take a break and come to dinner with my parents tomorrow night. They won't take no for an answer."

"That I *will* do."

Naomi started folding the clothes that Lisa was tossing onto the bed. And as they were packing, Evan started to cry.

"Oh, no. I'd better go to him. He's teething again."

"I'll go. You keep packing," Naomi said.

"Are you sure?"

"Of course."

Naomi slipped out of the room and went quietly into the baby's nursery. His cheeks were bright red and he was flushed. He stopped crying when he caught sight of her and looked up at her, his eyes moist with tears and his bottom lip sticking out.

"You're not feeling well, are you?"

Naomi held out her arms and the baby held up his. She picked him up and Evangelos settled right into the crook of her neck, stuffing a fist into his mouth and whimpering, his chest heaving.

Her heart melted as she held him, rubbing his back and swaying. Tears stung her eyes as she thought of her own baby. How she hadn't been able to hold him… or her.

But she couldn't deny that it felt nice to hold Chris's child close to her, and she made her way over to a rocking chair and sat down. Evan was startled for a moment but settled when he realized that she wasn't putting him down or leaving. That she was going to rock him and savor a moment that had been taken away from her.

Chris had heard the baby stir and start to cry. He knew that Lisa would be busy packing, so he went upstairs to calm his son down.

He saw that Naomi was holding him. She was swaying back and forth in the rocking chair as if it was natural to her, and Evan looked so calm, so peaceful in her arms.

A pang of longing went through him, making him deeply regret what he'd done to her years ago. How he'd messed up his own life in the process.

Why can't you have her? Why can't you marry her?

He shook that thought from his head. He'd hurt Naomi too much, and she'd made it perfectly clear that she just wanted to be friends with him. And even though in this stolen moment she was calming his son, he wasn't sure that she wanted that kind of responsibility full-time.

She had a good position now—who said she'd want to give it up to live with him and Evan here in Mythelios? That was if he even stayed here, because his life was in such a state of flux right now that he wasn't sure *what* he wanted at the moment. He wouldn't hold her back from her career.

I want this.

Only, he didn't deserve this, and he wouldn't ruin Naomi's life by saddling her with himself and Evan. And he wouldn't hurt his son by bringing someone into his life who might leave.

Chris clearly remembered how he'd felt when his

mother had left him. How it had completely crushed him… No, he wouldn't do that to his child.

He slipped into the room, breaking the spell. "Naomi, we have to go if we want to catch the ferry to Athens."

The baby stirred at his voice and held out his arms for him. Chris bent down and took his son from Naomi.

"Okay—what do you need help with?" She got up out of the rocking chair.

"I'll get Evan into his stroller, and if you can push him, then Lisa and I can handle the rest of the luggage. It's only a short walk down to the ferry."

"Sure." Naomi followed him out of the room.

Evangelos was fussing again, so before Chris got him into his stroller he gave him some more acetaminophen for the pain and then handed him a chilled teething ring to chew on.

Naomi managed the stroller, with the diaper bag and her own purse stowed underneath, Lisa had one small suitcase strapped to the top of the baby's case and Chris had a couple of suitcases too.

He locked up his *yia-yia's* house. Surprisingly, he was sad to leave it.

He didn't like the city anymore, but he had an apartment arranged for the next few days, and his father's yachts were all in Athens. He would manage until this bachelor auction was done with.

The three of them looked quite the sight walking down to the ferry. But they were able to board first, because of Evan, and quickly got settled. Lisa watched the baby, who had drifted off to sleep in his stroller, and Naomi got up and decided to stretch her legs on deck as the ferry pulled out of the port.

Chris decided to join her. "What have you got

planned for tomorrow morning?" he asked as they walked around.

"Nothing at the moment. I'm taking the morning off before I go to the venue where the bachelor auction is being held in the afternoon. I need to check on a few things there. Then I'm having dinner at Lisa's parents' house, apparently."

"Tomorrow morning I'd like to look for a tuxedo. I'll have Evan with me, but I need to get it done and I would appreciate help. It's not exactly easy, shopping with a baby in tow."

"Sure—I can help you. Where should we meet?"

"I'll pick you up at your apartment. It isn't far from mine, and there are some good shops within walking distance."

"Sounds like a plan. You have everything figured out!"

"I like to plan in advance now. It makes things easier," he said.

"No more flying by the seat of your pants and living for the moment, then?"

"No, you can't do that with a kid."

Her expression softened. "You're a *good* father. Don't let your own father get inside your head. You're doing an awesome job with Evan. Especially for someone who always expressly said that he didn't want kids or a family."

"I'm sorry I said those things, but I really didn't want them at the time. I do regret that I hurt you, though."

Her cheeks bloomed pink. "It's in the past."

"I know, but…"

"It's in the past, where it belongs, and I don't want to talk about it anymore. We're friends, and I want it to stay that way," she said. "I'm going to head back inside now."

Naomi walked away rather quickly and Chris couldn't blame her.

He'd clearly ruined what they'd had. And he'd always regret that.

CHAPTER TEN

CHRIS WAITED OUTSIDE on the sidewalk under a shady olive tree. Evan was playing with one of the toys that was attached to his stroller while they waited outside Naomi's apartment.

It was already hot outside, and it wasn't even mid-morning. He wasn't looking forward to trying on tuxe-dos, but at least it would be air-conditioned in the stores.

Naomi had been unusually quiet after they'd got off the ferry. She'd helped them get a cab at Piraeus and told him she would see him tomorrow, but that had been it. Lisa had helped him get settled in the apartment with Evan and then had taken another cab to her parents' place for her days off.

Lisa had invited him and Evan to the dinner tonight, but he wasn't sure he should intrude on a family meal. Especially when things were slightly tense again be-tween him and Naomi. He didn't want her to think he was going where he wasn't wanted.

Naomi came outside and saw them waiting under the tree.

"I see you found a shady spot," she said, before crouching down to greet Evan with a warm smile and a gentle pinch of one chubby cheek.

"It's blistering out. This has been one of the hottest summers that I can remember in a long time."

"Well, let's get to a store that has air-conditioning."

"Agreed," Chris said, and he pushed the stroller along the sidewalk to where the shops were. Naomi was walking by his side and anyone who looked at them might think they were a little family.

It gave him a warm feeling inside.

Don't think like that.

"Have you spoken to Lisa this morning?" Chris asked.

"No. Why?" she said.

"She invited me to their family dinner tonight. Or rather me and Evan. Apparently her parents want to meet her employer and his son."

"That sounds like my uncle!" Naomi chuckled. "Are you going to come?"

"Do you *want* me to come?" Chris asked. "I don't want to intrude."

"You wouldn't be intruding. Come. If Lisa asked you and my uncle wants to meet you because you're Lisa's boss, then you and Evan need to come."

"Okay, we will. I just didn't want to make you uncomfortable."

"You won't," she said quickly, but she was not looking at him. "Here's the shop. I'll manage the baby and you try on tuxes."

Chris opened the door and they were hit with a heavenly blast of cool air as Naomi pushed the stroller inside the shop.

A clerk greeted them and Chris explained what he was looking for. He was whisked away to get measurements taken while Naomi took a seat with the baby.

Then Chris was given several off-the-rack designer tuxedos to try that would be tailored to fit him exactly.

Naomi waited, with Evangelos in her lap, as Chris went into one of the curtained rooms.

"I want to see them," she said as she held on to one of the baby's toys with one hand, keeping her other arm around him. "I don't want you to let down my carefully planned event!"

"Ha-ha," he responded as he put on the first tuxedo.

It was a bit too large, but he came out to show her nonetheless.

She wrinkled her nose. "No, that's not it."

"I didn't think so," Chris said. "I could get this done a lot faster if I didn't have to show you each one."

"What? It's nice in here. Don't rush."

He grinned at her and then headed back into the changing room. He repeated the process with two other tuxedos and finally tried on the last one—which was a particularly expensive designer.

As soon as he put it on, it looked almost as if it had been made for him. And it would need very little alteration. It had been a long time since he'd worn a tuxedo. It felt a bit odd to be wearing one now.

He stepped out of the changing room and Naomi raised her eyebrows. Evan clapped.

"Not bad," she said. "See—even your son agrees."

"He claps when I do the dishes. He'll clap at anything."

"It looks good," she said. "That's the one you need to get."

The clerk who had been hovering stepped forward. "It suits you very well. It just needs minor adjustments."

"Can you have it done by Friday morning?" Chris asked.

"Yes, of course, Dr. Moustakas. A lot of men have come here for the auction," the clerk said, pinning the tuxedo and making the adjustments.

"Is there a lot of buzz about it?" Naomi asked.

"A *lot* of buzz. The shop next door is selling many formal gowns. It will be a night of splendor."

Chris turned to Naomi. "I hope you have a dress."

"Of course. I'm the master of ceremonies for this thing. I got my dress a few days ago."

"You're a good planner," Chris teased, before he went back inside the curtained room to take off the tuxedo.

Once he'd changed out of the tuxedo and paid for it, with another guarantee from the clerk that it would be ready in time for the bachelor auction on Friday, he followed Naomi, who continued pushing the stroller as they left the store.

They walked along the sidewalk until they found a little park that was shady. Chris picked Evangelos up out of the stroller and took him over to one of the infant swings. Strapping him in, he began to push gently.

First Evan had a big grin on his face, and then he started to screech with laughter.

Naomi started laughing as well, and Chris couldn't help but smile too. When he was a kid, he'd never gone to a park. His father had always been too busy and the nannies who'd taken care of him had never taken him either, for some reason.

"Look at how much fun he's having," Naomi said. "It's adorable."

"It looks like fun," Chris said, pushing his still giggling son. "I've never been on a swing."

"What? Never?" Naomi asked, stunned.

"Nope. I didn't get to play in parks and there weren't any swings on Mythelios. I've swung on a rope before…"

"You were *so* deprived! I spent my summers in our local park. We'd stay out all day until the streetlights came on and then we'd head for home. Of course, it was different back then."

Chris nodded. "Well, I'm glad Evan is able to enjoy it."

Naomi glanced at her watch. "I have to get back to check on the venue."

"Do you want me to walk you to your apartment?" Chris asked, even though he wasn't sure he would be able to pull his son away from the swing.

"No, you stay here with Evan—he's having so much fun. I'll see you tonight."

Naomi waved at the baby and then walked out of the park, disappearing down a side street.

Evan looked after Naomi, his lip protruding, and began to fuss.

Chris stopped the swing and picked him up, holding him close. "Yeah, I miss her too."

He missed her so badly—but it was all his own fault. And he couldn't go back and fix his mistakes. No matter how much he wanted to.

Dealing with stuff at the venue had taken Naomi a bit longer than she'd expected, so now she was running late for dinner at her *theía* and *theíos's* house.

When she got to the house, her *theíos* Costa opened the door. "I thought you were lying dead in a gutter, Naomi!"

"I know I'm late, *Theíos*. Sorry, but there were some problems at the venue, and I'm not a party planner."

"You should've had your cousin Anita take care of that. She's a party planner."

"Isn't she on Mykonos?" Naomi asked.

Her uncle just waved his hand, as if it was no bother. "Family is family. Come into the living room. Lisa's boss, Dr. Moustakas, and his son are here. Lisa tells me you are friends with Dr. Moustakas?"

"Yes."

Her uncle grinned. "That is very nice indeed."

"No, *Theíos*, it's not like that at all."

Her uncle ignored her and led her into the large living room at the back of the house, which in turn opened out into the garden. Most of her cousins were there, and they greeted her with kisses and hugs as she came into the room.

Chris was sitting next to her *theía* Leda, who was holding Evangelos and making a fuss over him. Chris smiled at her and mouthed the words *help me* with a twinkle in his eyes.

Naomi couldn't help but laugh. Her father's family was loud, and very large, but they were warm and friendly. Still, she could see why her father had wanted to get away from it all. Her father had liked quiet. Maybe that was why she was an only child.

"Naomi, you didn't tell us what a nice man Dr. Moustakas is. Of course, Lisa didn't say either. And what a gorgeous baby he has!" her aunt gushed.

"You're very kind, Leda," said Chris.

Naomi took a seat next to him and reached out to touch one of Evan's chubby hands. "Where is Lisa?" she asked.

Leda leaned over Chris and said in a hushed tone, "Getting engaged. She's in the garden."

Naomi was shocked. *"What?"*

Leda nodded. "Her boyfriend, Themo, has been away for a year in America. He promised to come back, but Lisa didn't like to talk about it much, as she was hurt when he left. He returned yesterday and—well, you can't stop love."

On that bombshell, Leda handed the baby to Chris and moved away, leaving Naomi and Chris sitting there on the small couch looking stunned.

"I guess you're going to be looking for a new nanny soon," Naomi said. "I had no idea. She never even mentioned him to me."

"Me neither," Chris said. "Now I feel *really* bad, intruding on a family engagement."

"Don't feel bad. I don't think they knew it was coming when they invited us."

There was the sound of some excited voices and Naomi craned her neck to see over the heads of her family as Lisa and Themo came in together.

There were cheers as Lisa and Themo announced their engagement. Then ouzo was passed out on a tray, and everyone held up a glass in the air and drank in congratulation, with exuberant shouts of *"Opa!"* to follow, which caused Evangelos to cry.

Chris calmed his son, and Lisa came over with her new fiancé in tow.

"Themo, this is my cousin Dr. Naomi Hudson, who is visiting from America."

"A pleasure, Dr. Hudson," said Themo, taking her hand.

"And this is my employer, Dr. Moustakas, and his son, Evangelos."

Themo grinned and nodded as Chris stood, shifting Evan onto his hip in order to congratulate them both.

"Now I feel bad that I'm making you come back to work for the weekend," Chris said. "You should be celebrating with your fiancé, Lisa."

"No, it's no problem, Dr. Moustakas. Themo needs

to head back to Corfu to visit his family this weekend. We'll see each other next week, and we'll talk about my notice at the end of the month."

Chris nodded. "I'll hate to lose you, but I understand."

"Dinner is ready!" her uncle announced over the din.

Lisa reached out and took Evangelos. "You enjoy your dinner, Chris. I have an old high chair by me."

Lisa winked at Naomi and she felt heat rise in her cheeks. Evan was taken down to one end of the table and Chris and Naomi were seated at the other.

"I'm not used to this," Naomi whispered as Chris pulled out her chair.

"Me neither," Chris remarked. "I just have my father to deal with. Sometimes I go to dinner at Ares's place, or Theo's or Deakin's, but I don't remember it being such a crush of people like this."

"My father's family is quite large. My dad was always quiet, though, so I get why he went to America."

"And you said your *yia-yia* was a bit crazy?"

Naomi laughed. "Yes, but I wasn't the only one who thought that."

"You mean my mother?" her uncle Gus called from the other end of the table. "If so, yes—she *was* crazy. She was a crazy woman. You're not the only granddaughter she said was cursed, you know. She said Anita was cursed too, but she's married and happy in Mykonos. You will be announcing *your* engagement soon enough, Naomi."

Oh, Lord.

"Thanks, *Theios*."

Chris was chuckling as food was passed around the table. "You're *cursed*?"

"So said my late grandmother. She said I was cursed when I was about fourteen."

"And do you believe her?"

"I did."

That sobered him. "I don't think you're cursed. If anyone is cursed, it's me. But I don't like talking about curses too much—especially when I have to do some rounds at your hospital here tomorrow and now that Deakin has called. Stavros has agreed to surgery to remove the anaplastic oligodendroglioma."

"He has?" Naomi asked in shock.

"His brother is flying in from Venice to run the *taverna* for him while he recovers. It's going to be hard on Stavros. He's not a young man anymore."

"But he's not old either," she said. "Fifty-five isn't old. And he's in good health otherwise. He'll pull through."

"I know he will, but we have to convince Stavros of that. He wants the surgery done as soon as possible, so I've extended my stay in Athens. After the auction date night I'll have Stavros come to Athens so I can do it then. He won't wait."

"Good. Get it over and done with. And since you're here you might as well do it."

"Will you assist?" he asked. "I'm still not used to the surgical team here, and even though they're good, I would feel better if you were in the operating room with me. I trust you."

A pang of guilt cut through her. He shouldn't trust her—especially when she couldn't even tell him about the baby that she'd lost.

"Of course. I'll help any way that I can," she said.

"Good. I'm glad. I think I can pull it off, knowing that you're by my side."

She was stunned that he'd say that, because he would

never have said anything like that years ago, when they were dating. He had been full of himself then. Border-line arrogant. He'd walked the halls of the Nashville hospital where they'd met like he owned the place.

His absolute confidence and self-reliance was what had drawn her to him then, but *this* man, the way he was right now—still strong, still confident, but far more gracious and seemingly unafraid to admit to needing someone—was the kind of man she wanted.

He was breaking through all the barriers she had set up to keep him at bay. And as she glanced down the table at her big Greek family, seeing Evangelos next to Lisa, it was as if Chris belonged there. She felt as if *she* belonged there too. It was like they had been part of a great big family for a long time.

It scared her, but it also made her feel good.

After the death of her mother she hadn't been sure where she belonged. Chris had come along and swept her off her feet. And then he'd broken her heart. She'd been lost again. Just drifting.

Coming here to help after the earthquake had given her purpose, and being here, right now, with her fa-ther's family and with Chris, just seemed *right*. As it was supposed to be.

Only, it's not. You're just friends. Remember?

She was being swept up in the excitement of Lisa's engagement to her beau. That was all it was. There was an energy in the air tonight, and definitely romance, and Naomi had always been a sucker for happily-ever-after.

She was just being carried away. That was all.

Chris was chatting with another one of her uncles, so she ate her dinner, enjoying the fifty different conver-sations that were being blasted around the table, along with the hand gestures that seemed to accompany all the talking.

She couldn't help but smile. She was going to miss all this when she had to head back to America after her assignment in Athens was up, but at least she got to enjoy it now. And she was going to relish it.

After dinner was over, Chris managed to collect his son from his adoring fans and a cab was called. Evan was sleeping on his father's shoulder, tired out from all the attention and the excitement of the night. Naomi walked him to the door, pushing the empty stroller out onto the street to the waiting cab, while Lisa put the car seat in the back.

"Thank you for having me," Chris said to Naomi.

"I didn't have you—Lisa invited you."

"Yes, I've thanked her too. But I wanted to thank you for letting me come tonight. It was nice."

"I'm glad you came," she whispered. "I'll see you tomorrow at the hospital. And tomorrow afternoon is a dry run of the auction down at the venue."

"A rehearsal?" Chris shuddered. "Okay, I'll see you tomorrow at the hospital, then."

And then, before she knew what was happening, he leaned in and kissed her on the cheek, before climbing into the cab next to his son.

Naomi stood there, her pulse racing, stunned.

She was going to have to be more careful when it came to Dr. Moustakas or she would be in danger of losing her heart again.

Isn't it lost already?

CHAPTER ELEVEN

FRIDAY CAME AROUND all too quickly. Naomi had managed to avoid Chris all of Thursday. She'd been busy with things at the hospital and had stayed out of his way. Even during the rehearsal of the bachelor auction she'd remained backstage while the stage director had done his job in guiding some of Athens's most eligible bachelors across the stage and down to the table they were to be seated at after they'd been won by the highest bidder.

After the auction was over, there was going to be a "mix and mingle" for the rest of the evening, so plans for the dates they were planning could be settled by the bachelors and the ladies who'd won them.

Chris had looked confident onstage, but also a little flustered. She could only assume that it had been a long time since he'd done anything like that, or been the center of attention the way he had in Nashville, when he'd been the chosen one of the surgical fellows there. Or when he was in Manhattan, being feted by the elite of New York.

Or so she'd understood from the gossip magazines, which had featured him dating all the glitterati of Manhattan.

And now he was one of the most eligible bachelors in Athens. All the wealthy women attending this event would have eyes for Dr. Chris Moustakas. Not only was he famous for being the son of Nikos Moustakas, shipping magnate, but he was also well-known among the jet-setters for his brilliance in neurosurgery.

To top all that off, he was good-looking and he oozed sex appeal. He was a total catch. And Naomi was feeling a bit jealous that someone else would be winning a dream date with him. A dream date that she wouldn't mind going on herself.

He'd changed from the man she knew three years ago. He was kinder, more gentle, and the way he was with his son made her heart melt. This man, the way he was now, was the man she'd thought he was three years ago.

Careful.

She couldn't let him interfere with her life plans. She'd worked too hard to get where she was. It was good that she wouldn't have a chance to bid on him. Even if she wanted to.

Don't think about it.

Naomi sighed and finished doing her makeup. She had to be at the venue soon, to wrangle all the bachelors and make sure that she had the right descriptions for each one and details of the date that could be won.

She looked at her watch and then there was a buzz up to her apartment.

Drat. The limo had arrived to take her to the venue.

"I'll be down in a moment."

"Very good," the driver responded.

Naomi finished what she was doing and checked herself in the mirror. She was wearing a gold lace evening gown that was fitted, short and very sparkly. She was glad she was getting a ride and that she could wear her heels tonight. She'd left her hair down.

She hoped she was representing International Relief well enough tonight. And she hoped she'd make a good impression on the hospital's board of directors.

She ran her hand over her dress and then headed downstairs. The driver helped her into the limo. Her heart was hammering, because she hated public speaking. She pulled out her cards about the dates and the bachelors, reading them through once again.

You can do this.

It didn't take long until they were at the outdoor venue. Thankfully it was a beautiful clear evening. She was led to the front. People were starting to arrive and there were pictures being taken of all the attendees of the gala on a red carpet.

"Dr. Hudson, I would like you to meet someone," said Mr. Galinakas, the head of the hospital board, as he led her off the red carpet to a group of women who were dressed to the nines in designer gowns.

It made Naomi feel she wasn't up to muster—but only for a moment. She knew she looked just as good as they did.

"This is one of our benefactors, Ms. Alexandra Pappas."

Even during her short time in Athens Naomi had heard of Alexandra Pappas. She was a gold digger. She'd been married four times to wealthy older men and had outlived them all. She had a penchant for playing with younger men but marrying older ones. She was a maneater, a manipulator, and Naomi couldn't help but think of Evan's mother, who had only wanted money to have a baby.

Alexandra Pappas held out her hand as if she was bestowing some great honor on Naomi. But Naomi could see right through this woman.

"Charmed," Alexandra drawled in a bored tone.

"Alexandra is looking forward to bidding tonight," Mr. Galinakas said.

"Oh?"

"Yes. I was widowed last year and I'm looking for the right companion. I think this is a wonderful idea and there is one bachelor I have my eye on. One I haven't seen in our social circles in quite some time."

Naomi's stomach knotted as she realized exactly who Alexandra was talking about. She was referring to Chris.

"Well, it's a pleasure to meet you." Naomi glanced over her shoulder to see the stage director motioning toward her. "I'd better go. It's almost showtime."

The director came over and she was led to the back, where about twenty very handsome and eligible men, all wearing gorgeous tuxedos, were milling about and chatting.

"Hey, y'all!" Naomi called out, her Southern accent getting thick because she was nervous. "Thank you for coming and donating your time to this worthy cause."

There was applause, and she scanned the crowd of men until her gaze landed on the one man she was looking for. Her heart skipped a beat. He stood there grinning at her, his hands in the pockets of the expensive tuxedo that fitted him in all the right places. He winked at her, his dark eyes glittering with mischief—and something else that made her weak in the knees.

Focus.

"We're going to get started in a moment. I'll be talking you up to all those who are bidding on the date, and my friend Antreas here will be taking the bids."

Antreas bowed and spoke a few words while Naomi

tried to regain control of her nerves. She was suddenly sweltering in her designer gown.

"They're ready," the stage director said. "You're up, Dr. Hudson. They're about to introduce you."

"Okay."

She took a deep breath and climbed the stairs behind the stage, waiting until the chief of the board of directors announced her. There was applause as she crossed the stage and made her way to the podium, with Antreas trailing behind her.

When the applause died down, she took one of the microphones handed to her and gave Antreas the other.

"Welcome, everyone, and thank you for supporting International Relief's bachelor auction. The money from tonight will be used to help earthquake victims on Mythelios as well as those who were brought to the hospital here in Athens for treatment. It will also go toward replacing damaged equipment at the Mythelios Free Clinic."

There was another round of applause.

"All the bachelors here tonight are from Athens and the surrounding islands, and we have thirty-five eligible men taking part! They have generously donated their time and money to give someone a great date night. Antreas Satros will be conducting the auction and taking your bids. I hope you all have your paddles. If you win a date with one of our bachelors, please hand in your paddle and give your information to our lovely ladies in the back. You'll have time to meet with our bachelors after the auction, during our mix and mingle. All dates will take place tomorrow night. Now, are we ready to get started?"

There were cheers from the crowd and she could feel

her heart pounding loudly between her ears as she plastered a fake smile on her face.

"Without further ado, please welcome our first bachelor of the evening. Taki Hatzidou—a real estate magnate from Athens."

Taki, a tall Greek god with blond hair, came out onto the stage and flashed a brilliant smile under the bright lights. He winked at Naomi and openly flirted with her, and she played right along.

"Your date with Taki will involve a night of luxury in Athens. A private evening dinner atop the Acropolis, a helicopter ride and dancing under the stars. We'll start the bidding at ten thousand dollars. Remember, this is in US currency!"

It didn't take long before the date with Taki Hatzidou was won by someone bidding well over eighteen thousand dollars, and Naomi announced the next bachelor.

As the bachelors came out on stage in turn they all flirted with her. It was working well, and Naomi soon found herself in a bit of a groove and started enjoying herself.

"Now for bachelor number ten…" She trailed off as she realized it was time to auction off Chris in front of the hungry hordes of single wealthy females who wanted to win a date with him. "Dr. Christos Moustakas—world-renowned neurosurgeon and native of Mythelios."

Chris came out on stage, looking mighty sexy and svelte in his designer tuxedo.

"Your date with Dr. Moustakas will involve a ride on one of the Mopaxeni yachts under the stars to the small island of Spritos, where dinner will await at the private beachfront property of shipping magnate Nikos Moustakas, who happens to be Dr. Moustakas's father, well-known in Athens's social circles. We'll start the bidding at ten thousand."

In a flurry, multiple paddles were raised, and Chris shot her a flirty glance, just like all the other men had done before.

Then Alexandra Pappas stepped forward and raised her paddle. "Fifteen thousand!"

Naomi's stomach twisted.

There was another flurry of bidding and then Alexandra shouted out, "Twenty thousand!"

Chris was flirting with Alexandra too, as he was supposed to do.

Before Naomi knew what she was doing, she shouted out, "Twenty-one thousand!"

Antreas was taken aback, but he continued taking bids and Naomi kept bidding.

Chris was still smiling, but she could see the surprise on his face. She was just as surprised at herself—but she didn't want another woman to have a dream date night with Chris.

The crowd seemed to love the fact that the master of ceremonies was getting in on the event and bidding.

It all came down to her and Alexandra Pappas—the Athenian socialite who had been married four times to wealthy men, who was a man-eater and who probably had way more money in the bank than Naomi.

But there was no way she was going to let that woman, dripping in diamonds, get her claws on Chris. Naomi had some money stashed away after a shrewd investment a few years back, and suddenly she felt compelled to dip into it. A *lot*...

"Twenty-five thousand!" Alexandra said, sounding smug but seeming to waver.

Naomi saw the look of concern in her eyes and knew

that she almost had her. "Twenty-six thousand!" she shouted.

"Twenty-seven!"

"Twenty-eight!" Naomi's pulse was thundering in her ears and she wasn't sure she was going to be able to maintain her grip on the microphone.

"Thirty thousand!"

"Thirty-five thousand!" Naomi shouted.

Chris's mouth dropped open—as did Antreas's.

The man-eater dropped her paddle and shook her head, but there was a look of venom pointed in Naomi's direction. She didn't care. She had kept that woman from getting her greedy hands on Chris.

"Going once...twice...and Dr. Naomi Hudson has won a date with Dr. Moustakas!" Antreas shouted.

There was loud cheering—because it was all for charity and for fun.

Naomi's hands were shaking as Chris came up beside her. He said nothing, just led her down the stairs and offstage. She had to go and give her information to the ladies at the back. And he walked with her.

One of the stagehands took her microphone and Antreas began to work the crowd and get them worked up for the rest of the bachelors.

Chris's arm slipped around her waist, steadying her. She was still in disbelief over what had just happened.

"You just bid thirty-five grand on me," he said.

"I know," she whispered, her voice shaking. "I'm in shock."

"You're not the only one—but I'm glad it was you who won the date with me," he said huskily in her ear.

Warmth spread through her body. "Me too."

"You look beautiful, by the way. Wear this tomorrow night and I'll wear my tuxedo. It's going to be a fantastic night."

He left her then, to return to where the other bachelors were standing. She was still shaking as she gave her information and wrote a large check.

She headed back to the stage when she'd regained her composure.

When she walked back onstage, everyone applauded her—including Chris, who was still standing in the bachelor holding area.

Focus.

She'd deal with the repercussions of her impulsivity later—tell herself that at least the money was going to a good cause.

"Right, so now that I'm completely broke, you ladies won't have to worry about me jumping the gun like that again. Y'all got me so excited I *had* to join in too."

There was laughter—except from Alexandra Pappas, who was still shooting daggers at her. Naomi had definitely dug her own grave within the Athens social circle. But she couldn't think about that right now—and she frankly didn't care. There was nothing in the contract that said she couldn't bid on a bachelor. It was for charity, and she'd won fair and square.

"So, bachelor number eleven—will you come up here, please? Bachelor number eleven is Petros Krivo, who is a surgeon at the hospital. He specializes in broken hearts…"

She glanced briefly over at Chris again, and he winked at her, but she looked away as Petros came onstage and bidding on him began.

Chris hadn't managed to get to Naomi after the bachelor auction was over. Everyone was congratulating her for a job well done, and for the amount of money she'd both donated and managed to raise.

She might not like public speaking, but she'd owned that crowd tonight. She'd been sexy, funny and vibrant as she'd announced the bachelors. And it had only made the event even more fun when she'd started bidding.

What had surprised him was that it had been on *him*—but it had also thrilled him. He knew the woman who had been trying to outbid Naomi, and he was glad that he wouldn't have to spend all of tomorrow night trying to fend her off.

Now he had to spend his date night trying very hard not to take Naomi in his arms and kiss her, as he'd been longing to do ever since he'd first laid eyes on her again in Mythelios. But he wouldn't hurt her. He couldn't do that to her again.

He smiled, watching her speak to all the bigwigs who were just *gushing.* They were putty in her hands and she had no idea.

When the crowd around her was finally relaxing a bit, he grabbed an extra glass of champagne from one of the side tables where it was being poured by the wait-staff and made his way over to her.

"Ah, the man of the hour," said the head of the board of directors at the hospital. "It really added to the excitement of the evening when Dr. Hudson bid on you."

Chris grinned. "Well, we do have a bit of a history. We were fellows together in Nashville, in America."

Naomi blushed and he handed her the glass of champagne.

"You're all to be congratulated for raising over eight hundred thousand dollars!"

"Yes—job well done, Dr. Hudson," said the head of the board, and the group that was still around Naomi applauded.

"If you don't mind, I would like to discuss with Dr. Hudson the details of our date tomorrow night."

"Not at all," said the head of the board.

Chris took Naomi's arm and led her away from the gaggle of people.

"Thank you for rescuing me. My face feels frozen from all the smiling."

Chris chuckled. "Have a glass of champagne—it'll help ease your nerves."

She took a sip. "I'm so glad you're not annoyed with me."

"Why would I be annoyed?" he asked.

"Because I won the date."

"I'm relieved. I know the woman who was trying to outdo you. I would have spent my entire evening trying to pry her tentacles off me."

Naomi laughed and took another sip. "Still, I'm glad you're okay with it."

"Are you looking forward to the date?" he asked.

"We don't have to go through with it."

"Nonsense—it's part of a charity event and you paid good money to be wined and dined. We're going."

"Okay…"

"I'll pick you up at six and then we'll take the yacht out for a cruise and head to Spritos for dinner on the beach. My father has lent me the use of his beach house for the evening."

"Sounds wonderful!" she gushed, and then she blushed.

He leaned in and whispered, "It *will* be wonderful."

Her blush deepened, and it took every piece of his self-control not to reach out and pull her into a kiss right then and there.

"You were amazing tonight, Naomi. Truly."

"Thank you. That means so much to me. I liked the way the bachelors all pretended to flirt with me—it seemed to get the bids up."

"Who said they were pretending?" Chris asked. "You were radiant out there tonight."

"Really?" she said, her breath hitching in her throat.

"Really." And then he couldn't help himself. He touched her face and leaned in, and he was just about to kiss her when Antreas the auctioneer came up.

"Dr. Hudson, there are some benefactors who wish to congratulate you."

Naomi took a step back and Chris dropped his hand.

"I'd better go. I'll talk to you later."

Chris nodded and Naomi made her way through the partygoers with Antreas to the far end of the ballroom. Chris watched her, his pulse thundering between his ears and his blood raging with a flame that could not be extinguished.

He wanted her desperately—but then again, he'd never stopped wanting her. And tonight, with all those men openly flirting with her, he'd felt jealous, and angry at himself for letting her go three years ago.

What the hell had he been thinking?

You weren't thinking back then.

He had to get better control of himself. He couldn't lose his head like that again.

He finished the rest of his champagne and left the gala.

He'd see Naomi tomorrow night and give her a date she'd always remember.

One night. One stolen moment with her again before they went back to reality.

CHAPTER TWELVE

CHRIS WAITED IN the limousine for her. It had been the longest day of his life, and Evan had been extra-fussy, but Lisa was great at calming him down and she was thrilled that her cousin had won the date with him.

He had an inkling that Lisa was hoping that he and her cousin would get together, and he wondered how much Lisa knew of their story and if she would feel the same if she knew how he'd treated Naomi three years ago.

Don't think about it.

Naomi came out of the building. She was wearing another beautiful dress, with the shoes from last night that made her already long legs look even longer. The shimmering dress made her skin glow and, seeing the way it fit all her curves, he was instantly thrown back into the memory of what she looked like under her clothing, how she felt in his arms, how she tasted on his lips.

Don't think about it.

He got out of the limousine as she approached and opened the door for her.

"Thank you," she said, slipping in and sliding over to the far side.

"My pleasure." He got in beside her and shut the door.

Once the door was shut, the limo took the long route

down to the yacht club, where his father's yacht was waiting with a small crew to take them to Spritos.

"Is that champagne again?" she asked.

"Close—it's prosecco. Would you like a glass?"

"I would love one."

He handed her one of the flutes and saw her hand was shaking, as if she was nervous.

"You okay?" he asked, though deep down he was secretly pleased that she was as nervous as he was. The only time he'd been nervous around a woman was when he'd been with her.

It unnerved him how much he wanted her. Even after years apart.

"I'm fine," she said, her accent becoming thicker, which he found incredibly endearing. She took a sip. "This is really good. I think I like it better than champagne."

"The Italians will be pleased," he teased as he downed his own drink.

The limo wound its way through Athens, and they got glimpses of the Parthenon, but he was looking forward to their night's escape away from the city. Away from all the people so that it was just them.

The tension in the back of the limo was heavy, and he couldn't find the words to say to break it.

"How is the baby?" Naomi asked nervously.

"Fine... But if you don't mind, I don't really want to talk about him tonight."

This would be so much easier if she was a stranger. With a stranger he could chat about nothing and know that the night would not end up in his bed. Now he was fighting every instinct he knew not to seduce the only woman he'd ever cared for deeply.

Maybe he *should* talk about Evan, then at least it would distract him.

Only, he didn't want to talk about his son tonight. Tonight he didn't want to be a single father. Tonight he wanted to be the man he'd been before his son had come. Actually, scratch that, he wanted to be a better man than he had been before. Even if just for a night.

The limo parked at the docks and Chris got and went to the other side and opened her door, holding her hand to help her out. Her hand shook in his and he smiled at her. When she was standing, he brought her hand to his lips and kissed it.

"What was that for?" she asked, surprised.

"It calmed you down, didn't it."

Naomi frowned but then laughed. "I suppose it did. I don't know what my problem is tonight. It's just you."

"Right. It's just me. And we know each other very well already. Just relax."

She nodded and he took her hand, leading her to the yacht. The captain was there to greet them, but he was quick about it because he already knew where they were going and what the plan was.

"This is a different yacht," Naomi remarked as they walked up from the main deck to the sun deck and into the living area. "It's larger than the one your father took me home in."

"That's his sport model. This yacht, *The Bella*, is his showpiece. He has an even bigger one."

"How many yachts does one man need?" Naomi asked.

"For my father—three. Boats are his thing. He is a part of Mopaxeni, after all."

"Which is how you met your friends who fund the clinic in Mythelios?"

Chris nodded. "When there were business meetings, we played together. I'm the eldest, and Ares is the youngest, but we formed a strong bond, and I think of them more as brothers than friends."

"And what did they think about you being in the bachelor auction?" Naomi asked, taking a seat on the leather couch.

"Ares was supposed to be taking part—I took his place when he found the love of his life. I suppose he owes me." Chris laughed and then went to the bar and poured them a glass of champagne. "It'll be a leisurely ride to Spritos."

"That's okay. I'm in no hurry. I think this will be wonderful."

"It will be." Chris brought her a flute. "This is champagne now, and not prosecco."

Naomi took a sip and Chris sat down next to her as the yacht pulled away from the Athens yacht club and headed out onto the calm sea.

They were trapped now.

As she'd realized that the yacht was leaving the dock, she'd become visibly nervous again and had thrown up a wall. He could feel it. Not that he blamed her.

"Come," he said, setting down his flute on the table and taking her empty one and setting it down too.

"What're we doing?"

"I'm taking you on a tour."

"Oh, okay…"

Chris led her away from the living area and down the hall. "On this deck are four bedrooms. Each with its own bath. The deck below is for the crew, when my father goes on an extended vacation, and the galley, for when he has a chef onboard, so we won't go down there."

He opened the door at the end of the hall. "This is the master bedroom."

He ignored the fact that there was a large king-size bed in this berth. A bed that pretty much took up all the space.

"It's huge! I think it might be bigger than my whole apartment in Athens."

"My father likes luxury."

Chris shut the door quickly, because his thoughts had begun to wander to things it shouldn't. He led her up the stairs to the next deck.

"We have a fitness room and a games room on this deck, and outside there's a hot tub."

"Wow!"

"And up here," he said, leading her to the final deck at the very top, "is the bridge, and here we have the captain and his crew."

Captain Panos saluted and turned back to his work, and they headed down off the bridge, back to the original deck where they'd started from, and then wandered outside to where there was seating alongside the railing.

They sat down next to each other.

"It's a bit chilly out here with the sea breeze," she said, wrapping her arms around herself.

Chris stood and took off his jacket, arranged it around her. "There—that's better."

"Thank you," she said. "It's a beautiful evening and it looks like we'll be in for a spectacular sunset."

"Why did you outbid that woman for a date with me?" Chris asked. "After everything I did to you… Why?"

"I don't know," she said. "I honestly didn't expect to do it, but then I saw her, and I know her reputation.

I guess I got jealous. Which is foolish, since…" She trailed off and looked away.

"I'm sorry I left you like that," he said.

"Are you?"

He nodded. "It was the worst mistake of my life."

"You had an incredible job offer—you had to go."

"But in retrospect I should've taken you with me." He reached out and touched her face, moving closer to her. "Leaving you like that is something I've always regretted. Especially when I heard that you'd found happiness with another man."

"You never wanted to get married and I understand that." Then she shook her head. "Happiness with another man? Who? I never seriously dated again after you left."

Now he was shocked. "I heard that you had taken up with Dr. Robertson after I left and that you two were serious."

Naomi snorted. "He wished… No, I accepted a general surgery fellowship after you left, but then I had to take a bit of time off when…"

She got up and moved away agitatedly.

"When what?"

She was clearly holding back something of significance. Chris went to her and took her hands, but she wouldn't look at him.

"What happened? What are you not telling me? You've tried to tell me this before, I think, but always stopped yourself."

There were tears in her eyes. "I was pregnant with your baby when you left. I didn't realize at the time, but as soon as I did, I tried to contact you, to tell you. But you were gone and you wouldn't return my calls. Then I saw you in all the gossip papers, living this crazy, fast, jet-setting life. Early in my second trimester I miscarried and lost the baby. It crushed me, and I hated you for it."

His heart sank to the soles of his feet and he felt horrible.

He was a monster.

He'd been such a stupid fool.

All he could do now was hold her as she cried and whisper how sorry he was for leaving her like that. She'd been all alone.

"I'm so sorry I wasn't there for you."

"I know," she said finally, drying her tears. "I hated you for so long, but you were a different person back then. You've changed for the better."

"Have I?" he asked, ashamed of who he'd been back then.

"Of course you have." She touched his cheek. "I'm glad we're friends again. I'm glad I was finally able to tell you. It's a huge relief, to be honest."

He touched the hand on his cheek. "I'm happy that you did."

"I think I ruined our evening." Her voice wobbled with more unshed tears.

"No, you didn't. Now I know and there are no more secrets between us. Let's just enjoy the rest of the date."

She nodded, and when the yacht docked at his father's beach house on Spritos, Chris led her down the dock and past the house, and then down some winding stairs that led to the other side of the private cove to a hidden white sandy beach.

Staff had set up a table and chairs, but other than a couple of waiters they were alone on the beach, surrounded by high cliffs and the sheltered cove of calm turquoise sea—even though it was getting hard to see the exact color of the water as the sun had started to set in spectacular fashion.

He held out a seat for her and then sat down opposite.

They had a scrumptious dinner and chatted about work, but it was when the waitstaff had left and returned to the yacht and they were alone that Chris started to feel that nervous energy again.

He felt so terrible for leaving her. If he'd known that she was pregnant, he would never have left—but, being the person he had been back then, he probably would have resented her for holding him back, and he hated himself for that.

Except the difference was that Naomi wasn't like Evan's mother. She wouldn't have tried to blackmail him. He would have had a true partner to parent his child with.

"This has been the perfect night—except for when I almost ruined it," she said. "I just couldn't hide it from you anymore."

"I told you—you didn't ruin the night, and thank you for telling me. I needed to know the truth and I'm sorry I wasn't there for you."

"You're forgiven."

She smiled at him, and in the flickering torchlight she glowed. Why had he ever left her behind? What an utter fool he was.

"I was offered a new position today," she said, looking away.

His heart sank. "Oh?"

"A position in Houston, and I think I'm going to take it. It's my dream job. I would be the head of general surgery."

"Then you should take it," he said immediately. "You can't pass that up."

He couldn't hold her back. Not this time. He was truly happy for her, even though part of him didn't want to let her go.

She nodded.

"Would you like to dance?" he asked.

"There's no music," she said, laughing.

"Come on." He stood up and held out his hand.

She kicked off her heels and took his hand and he pulled her close, leading her in a silent dance in the moonlight. He was going to miss her so badly when she left, but he had to let her go. She deserved happiness and a chance at her dreams.

"What're you thinking about?" she asked, her eyes glittering in the darkness.

"How much I would like to kiss you, but that I don't deserve to."

Her heart skipped a beat and her blood heated. She was so close to him, her arms around him, and she couldn't believe that he was saying these things to her. He'd changed so much, and all evening she'd been fighting the urge to kiss him herself.

She didn't know what she'd been thinking when she'd outbid that woman last night, but now that she was here with him something had changed, and she knew she was falling in love again. She was falling in love with the new Chris even more deeply than she had with the man she'd used to know.

"Pardon?" she asked, finding her voice. Her hand trembled in his as they stopped dancing to the silent music he had been leading her in and took a small step back from one another.

"I said I would like to kiss you, but that I don't deserve such an honor. Not after the way I hurt you."

"That's in the past now," she said shakily.

"Is it?"

She nodded. "You *do* deserve it and I would like it very much if you kissed me again."

"Even though it can only be just this one night?"

She nodded. "Yes."

And as he leaned in she closed her eyes, his hands on her face as he finally kissed her again. It all came flooding back like a dream—how he fired her senses, her blood, and how she melted when she was in his arms.

The kiss deepened and her arms wrapped around his neck to hold him close once more as his hands slipped into her hair. She pressed her body closer, wanting nothing separating them. All she wanted was to be with him again. To give all of herself to him again, even if just for one night.

He scooped her up in his arms and she laughed as he carried her up the steps to the beach house.

"What will the staff say on the yacht?" she teased as he hurriedly pulled off his jacket and tossed it on the beach house floor.

"They won't pay any attention. They know the yacht is docked here for the evening. Besides, I'm giving you a tour of the beach house."

There was a twinkle of mischievousness in his eyes as he took her hand and led her upstairs, straight to the bedroom that faced the opposite side of the island, away from the yacht.

He kissed her again, urgently, and she melted into him.

Even though she'd sworn that she would never be with him again, she couldn't help herself. Other than a few odd dates now and then, there had never been a man in her life like Chris. And even though she loved him and couldn't have him, he was the only man she wanted.

She was a fool, but she didn't care at this moment of being in his arms. Her heart raced, adrenaline and passion coursing through her. She wanted to be with Chris again. Even if it was only for this one night. If she didn't take this chance, she'd always wonder *what if?*

She'd never be able to lay the ghost of Christos Moustakas to rest. He'd always be there, haunting her life.

"Are you sure, *zoi mou*?" he asked, resting his forehead against hers, his breath hot on her neck.

"I'm sure."

She kissed him passionately, letting him know how much she wanted him. She wanted to be lost in his arms one more time. His arms went around her, lifting her up on tiptoe as their tongues entwined in a deep kiss. His hands were like fire on her bare back.

This intense passion was something she'd only experienced with Chris. There had been no other man who had made her feel this way, and she knew there never would be.

The kiss ended and she could barely catch her breath. Her body was quivering with desire.

He stroked her face again. He wanted her just as much as she wanted him. He pushed her toward the bed and then he was behind her, undoing the clasp of her dress and pulling down the zipper at the back of it. Once the dress was undone, he ran his strong hands slowly over her shoulders, pushing it down and off. It pooled at her feet.

"Zoi mou," he murmured again, pressing a kiss on the sensitive nape of her neck, pushing back her hair to do so.

He ran his hand down the side of her body, his hand resting on her hip as she looked over her shoulder at him. Their gazes locked and emotion overcame her. A tear slipped down her cheek and he turned her around, cupping her face.

"Don't cry, *zoi mou*." He wiped the tears away with his thumb.

"Kiss me again, then," she whispered.

Chris obeyed, his mouth urgent against hers as he drew her body flush with his. She began to undress him, wanting nothing between them. There was no turning back and she didn't want to.

She slowly undid his bow tie and then his shirt buttons so she could run her hands over his bare chest. He moaned as she touched him.

His arms wrapped around her and he undid her bustier. When it dropped away, his kisses trailed down from her mouth over her body to her breasts. She gasped at the feeling of his tongue on one of her nipples. It ignited her blood like fire.

"Wait…" she murmured through the fog of pleasure. "Protection?"

"Don't worry. I have it." And he grinned in that cheeky way she so loved.

"Thank the Lord," she whispered, and pulled him down to the bed.

He pulled off his shirt and then his trousers. Then he came back and slipped off her underwear. She trembled at the touch of his hands against her thighs.

"Don't be nervous," he whispered in her ear. "It's only me."

"That's why I am nervous—*because* it's you."

He stroked her cheek and kissed her again, his hand moving between her legs. Her body burned with desire.

She arched against his fingers, wanting more. Wanting him buried inside her.

Their gazes locked and he shifted. He entered her and she cried out at the sensation of him filling her. He kissed her and began to move gently, slowly, taking his time when all she wanted was for him to possess her. To take her hard and fast. Her body had woken up after a long sleep. She wanted all of him and she wanted him again and again.

He quickened his pace in response to her pleading. It was primal and urgent. She came, a heady pleasure flooding through her body, and she dug her nails into his shoulders, holding him tight, her legs wrapped around his waist. Chris followed soon after, his head resting on her shoulder as he caught his breath.

He rolled away but pulled her with him. She clung to him, felt his hand stroking her back as she listened to his heart beating.

She was awake again, and all she could do was try to hold back the tears that were threatening to come. She wanted more time with him, but that could never be. She couldn't risk her heart again.

But you already did.

She shook away that thought and held tight to what was left of the night and these stolen hours with the only man she would ever love.

CHAPTER THIRTEEN

CHRIS DIDN'T WANT to let her go.

For a few brief, glorious hours he'd been just himself again. He wasn't a tired single father but the passionate man he'd once been. Only slightly different—because the old him would have walked away and not have felt as horrible as he felt right now.

She'd been pregnant and he hadn't been there for her when she'd lost the baby.

His baby.

He was a monster for sending her away. For not answering her calls when she'd phoned him a month after they'd parted. Now he knew why she had been trying to reach him and he loathed himself for freezing her out like that. He'd felt that a clean break would be kinder for them both, but he'd been so wrong. He'd never been the same man after he'd left her.

This crushing sense of guilt was something he deserved, and he only wished he could make it up to her. He wanted more time with her to do that, but she'd be leaving for Houston soon and she hadn't invited him to go with her.

He couldn't get involved with her and he couldn't hold her back. Not after he'd brought her so much pain in the past. She'd been offered her dream job and she had to take it. He would make sure she did—even if it broke his heart to let her go.

He propped himself up on one shoulder and looked down at her. She was gazing up at him, her glorious hair fanned out on the pillow.

"What?" she asked.

"I was thinking we should probably get back to Athens, though I really don't want to go."

She sighed. "You're right."

"I have to prep for Stavros's surgery. He's at the hospital now. He was admitted around dinnertime and the surgery is in the afternoon."

"Do you still want me to assist?"

"Of course." He got up and hunted down his trousers, pulling them on.

Naomi was chuckling and he turned to look back at her as he picked up his shirt.

"What's so funny?" he asked.

"What is your father's maid going to say when she sees what's happened to this bed?"

He grinned at her. "Not much. Nothing out of the ordinary."

She made a face. "I don't want to think of your father bringing women here."

He laughed. "Then you shouldn't have asked. This *is* his private getaway from Athens, after all."

Naomi got dressed and he was sad that she was putting her clothes back on when their night had been so magical. He'd always treasure it. Their one stolen night.

You could have more.

He ignored that thought, because he *couldn't* have any more with her. Not after what he'd done to her. She'd told him her grandmother had said she was cursed, but maybe *he* was the cursed one. He certainly felt cursed in this moment.

"My shoes are still on the beach," she said.

"We'll get them."

She took his hand and he led her down the path, back to the little cove where everything had been cleaned up—including the torches. It was still and dark, the only light coming from the full moon that was fading slightly now as dawn was about to creep up on them.

"I think they must have taken them back to the yacht," he said. "If not, my father will find them and send them to me."

"Let's hope they're on the yacht. I'm tired of losing shoes in Greece."

He laughed and took her hand as they headed back to the docks and climbed the steps onto the yacht.

Her shoes were in the living room.

"Thank goodness!" she said as she slipped them back on.

"I'll tell the captain we're ready to leave."

He left the living area and headed up to the bridge. Captain Panos was waiting and Chris told him to take them back to Athens—but not the leisurely way this time. Then he headed back to Naomi, who was curled up on the couch, looking out over the water as the yacht started pulling away from Spritos.

He sat down next to her.

"I had a great time tonight," she said dreamily.

"Me too. Are you tired?" he asked.

"A bit."

He moved closer and she rested her head against him. He used the remote to dim the lights. She drifted off to sleep against him and he stroked her head, wishing he could have her, wishing that he deserved her. But he planned to stay in Mythelios and she clearly wanted more than that. She was entitled to follow her dream and excel at being the brilliant surgeon he knew she was.

He couldn't hold her back, like he had almost done before. He had to let her go.

Even though he knew it would kill him.

Chris couldn't sleep after he'd dropped Naomi off at her apartment. He went back to his own apartment to change and shower.

Once he'd checked on Lisa and Evangelos, both of whom were sleeping, he wrote Lisa a note to let her know that he was going to the hospital to check on Stavros and prepare to remove the anaplastic oligodendroglioma from his temporal lobe and the part of the cerebellum where it had infiltrated.

It was a risky surgery for Stavros, but he was in good health for a man in his midfifties. Chris had already warned Stavros that it would be some time before he'd be back working at the *taverna*, but Stavros's wife, Maria, and his brother from Italy would be able to help him to keep his business going.

Chris had told Stavros it was now or never. Chris had to get it out before the tumor spread to more parts of his body. Once it started spreading, there was no point in doing the surgery. There was very little they would be able to do by then.

As he sat in an empty skills lab, he couldn't focus on the scans in front of him. All he could think about was Naomi and asking her to stay in Greece so they could see if it would work out between them this time.

But that was selfish of him and it made him angry.

He was a fool.

And he hated himself. Maybe it would've been better if she'd never walked back into his life. Then at least he wouldn't be so distracted by her now.

He swore and scrubbed a hand over his face as he leaned back in the chair.

He had to get Naomi out of his head.

There was a knock at the door and he glanced over. Naomi was standing there, awkwardly hovering in the doorway in blue scrubs.

"I thought I'd find you here," she said.

"Yeah, I'm just putting together a game plan." He motioned to the seat next to him and she sat down and slipped him a cup. "Thanks."

He took a sip and found it was strong espresso.

"I've had about three," she said.

He chuckled. "Are you ready?"

"I'm ready."

"It's been a long time since I removed a grade three anaplastic oligodendroglioma."

"You can handle it. You're a neurosurgical god." She grinned at him.

"Let's not joke about the gods—especially not before surgery."

"Deal."

She stood up, and they walked together down the hall. Before they entered the surgical floor, they put on their surgical caps and took off their lab coats and headed into the scrub room.

Stavros was waiting for them in the operating room. He was still awake. The surgical team was waiting for Chris to finish scrubbing before they put Stavros under.

It wasn't the surgical team he was used to, but at least

he had Naomi by his side and he was used to working with her. She was his good luck charm and always had been when they had worked together in Nashville.

He was still angry at himself for throwing all that away.

Don't think about it now.

He finished scrubbing up and headed into the operating room, where a scrub nurse gowned and gloved him.

"How are you today, Stavros?" Chris called out as the final glove was pulled on and he made his way over to him.

"I could be a lot better," Stavros replied nervously. "I don't like the idea of someone messing with my brains. Although my wife would say that I didn't have many to begin with."

Chris grinned at him from behind his mask. "I am the best there is, Stavros."

"So Ares told me when he convinced me to get this done."

"I'll thank Ares for that later."

"This surgery will give me a shot at a longer life?" Stavros asked.

Chris nodded. "It will be a difficult recovery. I won't lie. Recovery from brain surgery is not easy. And it will be painful. But if we get it all out now, then it won't spread and it won't kill you."

Stavros gave him a brave smile. "Then I'm ready, Dr. Moustakas."

Chris nodded at the anesthesiologist, who put an oxygen mask over Stavros's face. Chris rolled his shoulders and closed his eyes, picturing the brain in his mind.

Naomi walked into the operating room then and he flicked open his eyes, calming down immediately. Her eyes crinkled, letting him know she was grinning at him behind her surgical mask.

You got this.

He bent down as the scrub nurse slipped on his glasses and then his headlamp. The surgical site was prepared. Stavros's hair had been shaved to expose the part where Chris would be cutting. Underneath it all there was a nasty tumor growing and destroying this man's life and he would get rid of it.

He'd cut it away—just like he had to do with Naomi. *He* was the nasty tumor that had been growing in her life, sucking away all her goodness and making her sad. And once this surgery was done, he had to let her go. He had to concentrate on raising his son.

He was no longer free, but Naomi could be.

He wasn't going to hold her back from her potential. It was the only thing he could do to make up for not being there when their child had been lost.

He would never forgive himself for that. He would never be able to make it up to her, but he could at least do this. He could cut her free so that she wouldn't have to look back at him and live a life full of regret. She could move on and be happy in her new job.

Without him.

"Scalpel, please," he said.

Something had changed with Chris, and Naomi wasn't sure what it was.

Stavros's surgery had gone off without a hitch. It had been long, but Stavros had pulled through—much to Maria's delight when they'd told her. It would be some time before he could head back to Mythelios, though.

There would be no cost to Stavros. After the success of the auction Chris had convinced the hospital board to offer their surgical team and the use of an operating room pro bono.

Naomi had absolutely loved her time in Greece. And if she were being totally honest with herself, the job offer in Houston wasn't looking as gleaming and shiny bright as she'd first thought.

Her parents were both gone, and her mother didn't have much family surviving in the United States, so there really was no one left for her there. She'd thrown herself into her work and travelling with International Relief these last few years, but here in Greece she'd found something more.

Don't be a fool. Don't give up all your plans on the off chance that Chris will want to be with you.

She remembered what had happened last time. There was still that nagging little bit of her that didn't quite trust Chris. And his noticeable distancing of himself from her, not only in the operating room but even before then, had set off her alarm bells.

He'd begun to pull away as soon as the yacht had docked at the yacht club in Athens and the limo had dropped her off at home. The sparkle, the twinkle that was usually in Chris's eyes had gone. He'd thrown up an invisible wall. Just like he had before he'd announced that he was taking that job in Manhattan and leaving her.

Back then he'd just ended it and walked away, and she wasn't sure that her heart could take him doing that to her again.

She needed to end it first.

So she should take that job in Houston and put some distance between her and Greece. Between her and Chris.

He was standing at the nurses' station of the post-anesthesia care unit, writing notes at Stavros's bedside. Her heart ached, because she wanted to stay with him and Evan forever. She just didn't know if that was what he wanted too.

And if he didn't want her, then she had to leave.

He glanced up, as if he'd sensed that someone was staring at him, and gave her a half smile and a wave before handing the chart off to a resident and coming to speak to her.

"How's Stavros?" she asked numbly as they walked away from the recovery unit so they could speak and not disrupt the recovering patients.

"He's doing good. He's stable, but still out of it. He's on a lot of painkillers. Once he goes up to the intensive care unit, Maria can be with him. I think she'll help just by being there. Once he's conscious, I'll be able to assess him."

"So you're staying in Athens a bit longer?"

He nodded. "Yeah. I am. And when I return to My-thelios, Lisa is going to stay in Athens. She wants to get married really soon, so I'm going to cut down my hours at the clinic so that I can spend more time with Evan."

"You're going to give up your career?" she asked, confused.

"It's just a job. I don't need it. I have enough money to take some time off and raise my son. Do what's right."

"That's very admirable of you, but you have such a talent. You should keep helping out at the clinic."

"I will—I'll just be cutting my hours." He ran his hand through his hair. "And how long are *you* staying in Athens?"

"I don't know," she said.

"You're not going to walk away from that job, are

you?" he asked in disbelief, and she heard a hint of censure there too.

"I haven't definitely decided on taking that job, actually."

"You'd be a fool to walk away from it."

"Why?" she asked hotly.

"It's your dream job. You *should* take it. International Relief is all well and good, but you're far too talented to stay with them. You could really make something of yourself."

"What if I want to stay here?"

"Why?" he asked bluntly. "There's nothing here for you."

It was like a slap to her face. "Isn't there?"

"No. There's not." He looked away, his face like thunder. "Nothing has changed for me, Naomi. I can't give you the life you should have. I'm sorry that I left you alone to deal with the loss of our baby—"

"Don't even *talk* about that," she snapped. "You don't have any right to talk about that to me."

"Please, Naomi, don't be a fool. Take the job in Houston. Don't waste your time on me. I'm never going to get married. *Never.*"

"So you've always said—but I don't understand why. You said you didn't want to have kids, yet you have a son."

"He was a mistake. But he's *my* mistake and I live with that by being the best father I can to him." He scrubbed a hand over his face. "Naomi, you deserve better than me. I'm sorry if I led you on."

Her spine stiffened. "You didn't lead me on. I guess I wanted to lay some ghosts to rest and I don't regret our time together. Now I can move forward and forget all about you."

She wanted to scream and cry, but he was just telling her the truth. It was only what she had been suspecting all along. At least now she finally had the answer to her question.

He might not be a playboy anymore, but he certainly had no interest in changing his bachelor status. His love affairs were brief and he moved on as soon as he could.

And she should finally move on too—even though her heart was broken once again. She wouldn't let it drag her down the way it had done in the past. She would walk away from Chris Moustakas now and never think of him again.

But as she turned away, an alarm went off and a nurse came running toward them.

"Dr. Moustakas—Stavros is stroking out!"

Chris cursed and ran after the nurse, and Naomi followed him. Stavros was in arrest.

Chris was shouting orders over the commotion and Naomi hung back for a few moments. There was nothing she could do—she would just be getting in the way. So she slipped away as soon as Chris had the situation well under control.

He didn't need her—he never had—and she would now be able to live her life knowing that Chris Moustakas hadn't changed.

Not really.

CHAPTER FOURTEEN

"SO THAT'S THE whole story," Naomi said, sitting on the bench next to Lisa, who had brought Evan out for a walk in the park.

"I *knew* there was something more than you two just being friends," Lisa said. "What a butt-head."

Naomi chuckled. "No, don't be mad. He has always been up front about the fact he never wanted to get married or have a family. I was the one who thought that love could change everything. And maybe that's my curse, as *Yia-yia* always said. Maybe my curse is believing too much in happily-ever-after even after not getting my own."

"*Yia-yia* was a drunk!" Lisa said crossly.

"What?" Naomi asked, laughing.

"It's true. She was always on the ouzo. You heard Uncle Gus say it the other night at my parents' house. *Yia-yia* was insane. You're not cursed—if anything, you're blessed. You're a brilliant surgeon. And I'm sorry, but Dr. Moustakas *does* love you. It's totally obvious to everybody. He's just too stubborn to see it."

"Well, I can't wait around for him to realize it—and you're not to say anything to him."

"I won't." Lisa laid her head against Naomi's shoulder. "I'm going to miss you when you go. Will you come back in a couple months for my wedding to Themo? I want you to be one of my bridesmaids."

"Of course! If I can spend thirty-five grand on a doomed date, I can buy a plane ticket to attend my favorite cousin's wedding."

"Us girls have to stick together. I wonder why your father didn't give you his last name."

"Well, technically my parents were never married. My mother was Catholic and Dad was Greek Orthodox, Neither one would convert, so they just lived in sin. I was baptized Greek Orthodox, but I took Mom's name when I started medical school. I couldn't have patients trying to say *your* last name."

"There's nothing wrong with Kokkinou!"

They both laughed together.

"I'm still going to miss you, Naomi, but if this job is your dream job, you need to go for it."

Naomi nodded and stared up at the brilliant blue sky. She didn't want to leave Greece. She wished she could stay there. But she didn't want to keep running into Chris. She would never be able to get over him if he was always there.

"Oh, look who's here," Lisa whispered.

Naomi looked up to see Chris heading toward them. "I have to go."

Lisa nodded and kissed her cheek.

Naomi got up and walked swiftly in the opposite direction.

"Naomi, wait!" Chris called out.

She closed her eyes and stopped.

Just keep going.

"What?" she asked, turning around. "I have a lot to do."

"I know. I just wanted to say that I'm sorry we're parting on these terms. I wanted us to be friends."

"I wanted us to be friends too, but it's just not possible. How is Stavros?" she asked, changing the subject because she was tired of talking about *them*.

"He'll pull through—but we won't know the extent of any cerebral damage until he wakes. For now, he's alive."

"Good," she said gently.

"Naomi, I don't want it to end like this."

"Like what? This is *exactly* the way you want it to end. I get it. You don't want a relationship and I do. We can't be friends and soon we won't even be colleagues. You won't have to worry about seeing me just around the corner."

He looked away, his hands jammed into his pockets. "Well, I wish you well in Houston."

"Thank you." Tears were threatening to spill over. "Give my best to Stavros and his wife. As well as the rest of them at the clinic on the island. I don't think I'll have time to go back."

"I will."

Naomi nodded and walked away from him. Tears were streaming down her face, but she wouldn't look back this time. She was tired of looking back. It was time to move forward. It was time to start anew.

And that wasn't with him.

Lisa had been giving him the stink eye ever since the encounter in the park and he deserved it. Completely.

When he'd seen Naomi in the park, all he'd wanted to do was take her in his arms and kiss her. He was so selfish. He couldn't keep on hurting her.

So he'd given Lisa the night off and she'd already left to go and spend it with Themo.

It was just him and Evan in the apartment.

As he watched his son sleep, he remembered how scared he'd been when he'd found out he was going to be a father. But he'd stepped up and taken care of the son whom he shared with a greedy, selfish woman who was not that different from his own mother.

And the one woman whom he'd loved had lost their baby.

It broke his heart.

He'd put her through so much pain. More than he'd realized.

He wanted to give her so much. He wanted to be with her. But even if he could deserve her, there was the worry that if it didn't work out between them Evan would be from a broken family... He couldn't do that to his son. The pain from when his own mother had left was still fresh. Like an unhealed scar. He was never going to let Evangelos experience that.

There was a knock at the door. Chris cursed and left his son's nursery and went to answer it. He peered out through the peephole and was taken aback to see his father standing there.

He opened the door. "What're you doing here?"

"Is that how you greet *all* your guests?"

"Unexpected ones, yes, and you are definitely un-expected." Chris stepped to the side to let his father in before shutting the door.

"Where is my grandson?" Nikos asked.

"Sleeping. What're you doing here, *Pateras*? You never just drop by."

"And *you* only come to see me if you need money." His father sighed. "I'm sorry."

Chris was even more taken aback. His father never apologized. Not for anything. He watched as his father took a seat on his couch, his head in his hands.

"What's wrong?" Chris asked.

"I want to talk to you about something. Dr. Hudson—is she the one?"

"The one what?"

"The one that got away—or rather that you threw away and then started a string of affairs in Manhattan afterward just to get over her."

"Why would you think that?" Chris asked.

"Because I have spies at my beach house and the maid told me the state of the bedroom the next day."

"Yes. She's the one I foolishly left to go and take a job in Manhattan. I thought she'd moved on with another man, but she hadn't. Instead, without knowing, I'd left her pregnant with my child and she lost it. I am the worst kind of person. You don't need to tell me about my recklessness. But I am doing right by my son. I'm taking my responsibility as a father seriously. I love Evangelos enough that I will walk away from the woman I love just in case it doesn't work out—and with my track record, why would it? I don't want my son to go through what I did when Mother left me."

His father sighed sadly. "Christos, she never wanted to marry me. We had an affair and you resulted from that. We married because we had to—her parents insisted and so did mine. Yes, she was a very selfish woman. She didn't want you and I begged her to keep you. She was totally miserable. She did not want to be a mother or a wife, so I let her go. It was me that got rid of *her*."

Chris sat down, stunned. "Did you love her?"

"I did. I loved her with all my heart. But she didn't

want me or the life we could have had together. However, it's plain to me that you want Naomi and she wants you."

Chris shook his head. "I've broken her heart too many times. She doesn't want me now. She has a brilliant job offer in Houston. And even if she didn't go back to America, what if it didn't work out between us? What if Evangelos got hurt? I don't want him to carry the pain of rejection around inside of him, crippling him like it has me."

"Christos, I'm sorry that your mother leaving you broke your heart. It killed me every day to know that I was the cause of your pain. That I'd sent your mother away. If you're going to blame someone, let it be me— but there's a huge difference between your mother and me and you and Naomi."

"Oh?" Chris asked. "What's that?"

"She loves you. Your mother never loved me. I understand the pain Naomi is feeling. She thinks that you don't love her and that's why she's going to Houston. I had to walk away from my marriage, and at the time I thought that I would eventually be able to move on from your mother. I tried, but it never worked. I could never lay the ghost of my unrequited love to rest. She was always there, haunting every aspect of my life. Including you—which was why I couldn't look at you. For that, Christos, I'm truly sorry."

Chris was stunned by his father's admission of the reason why he had been pushed away as a child by both his parents. Why his father had always been so cold and distant toward him.

"Don't make the same mistake as me, Christos. You love Naomi and she loves you. She would never leave you and Evangelos."

"She won't take me back. I hurt her too much this time. And she's taking her dream job in Houston. I can't force her to choose between me and her career."

"You're not forcing her if you give her a choice. Let her choose. Stop making decisions for the both of you. Besides, you could go with her, couldn't you? What's keeping you here in Greece?"

"The clinic—and I want to raise my son here..."

"Those are pathetic reasons, Christos. The clinic did just fine without you before, and I'm sure Ares, Deakin and Theo will all understand if you go with Naomi. Evangelos will always have a home here in Greece as you'll still have your *yia-yia's* home on Mythelios. I'll hire someone to watch it for you. But do go after Naomi before it's too late."

"And if she doesn't want me?" Chris asked numbly.

"Then at least you'll know. Just don't throw your chance of true happiness away, Christos. You've been given a second chance to make things right."

His father was right. He had been miserable about his decision not to pursue Naomi. And even though there was no certainty that Naomi would forgive him, or even agree to stay with him, he had to take the risk. He'd taken so many risks in his life leading up to this point—he couldn't not take this one. The greatest risk of all.

He had to put his heart on the line for the first time in his life. He had to take a chance on love, and on her, or he would live to regret it forever. And thinking about his life without her in it was just too much for him to handle.

His life had been so empty once before after he'd walked away from her.

It would be empty again if he let her go again now.

His father stood up and laid his hands on his shoulders. "Christos, please don't make the same mistake again."

"I won't. But I have the baby and…"

"I can stay with Evangelos."

Chris arched an eyebrow. "You?"

"I have a few things that I'm seeking forgiveness for. And spending time with my grandson is one way I can make amends. I'm sorry too, Christos. Very sorry. And I want you to know that I am very proud of you. I may have been disappointed with some of your choices in life, but I *am* proud of you. Don't throw away your love, your life *or* your career."

His father embraced him and Chris hugged his father for the first time in his life. He could feel the carefully constructed walls he'd built as a young child to protect himself from pain start to come crashing down.

"I'll be back as soon as I can!" Chris ran to the door and grabbed his keys. "There are bottles in the refrigerator and—"

"Would you go? It may be some time since I did it, but I do know how to take care of an infant. I'm the one who took care of *you*, after all."

Chris nodded and left the apartment.

He ran down the stairwell to the first floor and out into the street. His father's limousine was waiting outside for his father to return. The chauffeur stood up.

"Do you need to go somewhere, Dr. Moustakas?"

"Yeah, I need you to take me to someone's house. It's a bit narrow, down by Plaka, but if you could drop me off near there, I can walk."

The chauffeur nodded. "Of course."

Chris jumped into the front of the limo. His heart was hammering against his chest erratically as he thought about what he was about to do.

He only hoped that he could make everything right. That he could fix his mistake and that Naomi didn't completely hate him. That he hadn't blown his second chance with her...

Naomi stood in the small garden of her *theíos* and *theía's* house. She was staring up through a thick grove of olive trees at the moon. She'd come to say a final goodbye to her family.

Her *theíos* didn't understand why she was leaving, but she didn't want to get into it with him. She'd told her aunt and uncle that she'd gotten a really great job offer and that she couldn't pass up the opportunity to take the job. They'd accepted that.

She was just relieved that Lisa hadn't said anything to her parents about Chris.

Now she was waiting in the garden for her aunt to come back from a friend's so that she could say good-bye to her.

I don't really want to leave.

She wanted to stay here in Greece. She wanted to keep working for International Relief. The board of directors at the hospital in Athens had offered her a job as well—a position as the head of general surgery. It was just that Houston offered her a way to escape Chris.

Tears filled her eyes as once more she thought about him. About falling into the trap again. Except that she hadn't really fallen into the trap *again*; she'd been caught in it years ago. She'd never stopped loving him.

When she'd lost their baby and been so angry that he wasn't there for her, she'd still loved him. Even though she'd mourned their child by herself, when she'd seen him with his son, she'd loved him all the more, and she loved Evangelos too.

She loved Mythelios and her work there. She had family here in Athens. But she just couldn't stay. She couldn't watch Chris's life carry on without her. If she didn't leave, she'd never be free of him. Even if she didn't really want to be.

She had to go to Houston and maybe—just maybe—she'd be able to mend her heart properly this time and finally move on away from Chris. Maybe she would find some sort of happiness and break the curse of loving someone who clearly didn't love her back.

"Naomi?" her uncle said from the terrace door.

"Is *Theía* back yet?"

"No, but…"

He stepped out of the way and Chris walked out onto the terrace. Her heart skipped a beat.

"How did you know I was here?" she asked.

"I went to your apartment first, then the hospital, and then I came here. If you hadn't been here, I was going to go to the airport next."

"What are you doing here?" she asked.

"I came to talk to you." He looked uncomfortable. *Good.*

"I'll leave you two to it," her uncle said, shutting the terrace door as Chris stepped out into the garden with her.

She crossed her arms and waited for him to say something, but he didn't. He just stood there with his hands in his trouser pockets.

"What do you want, Chris? I have to go home and pack and—"

"I'm sorry, Naomi."

"So you've said several times before. You were sorry for leaving me the first time…sorry that I was left pregnant and you didn't know about it. You were sorry that

I lost the baby and you're sorry for breaking my heart again. I get it. You're sorry."

"Naomi—"

"No, I've heard it all. Haven't we said enough to each other? Why won't you let me go in peace?"

A tear slid down her cheek, but she always cried when she was angry, and she was mad that he was here apologizing to her yet again.

"I don't know what you think apologizing to me over and over again will accomplish. If it's to redeem your guilty conscience, don't feel guilty. I will be okay. Just go away and let me get on with my life."

"No," Chris said quickly.

"No?" she asked, her voice rising. "Why?"

"Because I'm a fool."

"That's an understatement."

He ran a hand through his hair. "I ran from any kind of commitment, any kind of love, because I was afraid of being hurt again. When my mother didn't want me, when she left, it crushed my soul. And I saw the way it hardened my father's heart. I didn't ever want to have that experience. I didn't believe in true love. But then I met you."

"Why are you trying to explain all this to me again? I get it, but it doesn't change how I feel. It doesn't change how you broke my heart. You don't know what I went through when I lost our child. You weren't there."

"I know," he said. "And it kills me that I wasn't there to be with you when I should've been. I love you so much, Naomi. I never did stop loving you. I thought that leaving you behind in Nashville would be the way I could get you out of my soul, but you stayed there, and when I thought you had taken up with someone else, it drove me mad, straight into the arms of an unworthy person—but at least she gave me Evan."

"All you had to do was call me back to find out what was going on with me, but you wouldn't answer my calls."

"Because I was a complete idiot. I wish that I could go back in time and kick my old self in the head for what I did to you, Naomi. I do. But this time around… I can't live without you, Naomi. I *won't* live without you. It scares me to my very core that I don't know what the future holds, and that it may never work out between us, but if I don't take the risk, I'll never know."

"What're you saying?" she asked brokenly.

"I'm saying that I want to make it up to you—if you'll let me."

She was stunned as he got down on one knee in the middle of her *theía* and *theíos's* garden and took her hand.

"I want to marry you, Naomi."

Her heart skipped a beat. She wasn't sure that she was hearing him right. "Pardon?"

"I want to marry you…if you'll have me. I may not have a ring, but I want to marry you and spend my life trying to make it up to you. I want to make a family with you and Evan. And I don't care where that family will be. We'll come to Houston with you. I just can't lose you again. Please—give me another chance. I was a fool, but there is no other that I love. I'll never love any other woman like I love you. You're *it* for me, and I can't live without you."

Tears streamed down her cheeks. "You crushed my heart…"

"And I will never forgive myself for that. But you have always had my heart safe in your keeping. I should have followed where my heart was leading me three years ago. I was a fool for trying to fight what I always wanted—and that was you."

She smiled. She couldn't believe the words that were coming out of his mouth. "I love you too. I always have. I've tried to move on, to forget you, but I can't."

"Is that a yes?"

"You'll go wherever I need to go? What about the clinic and the house?"

"They'll always be there, waiting for us, but this is *your* time to shine, Naomi. I just want to share in a bit of your sunlight."

He stood up and cupped her cheeks, wiping her tears away with his thumbs.

"I don't deserve you, but I promise I will make it up to you and be the man you need me to be."

"I love you too. Yes, I'll marry you."

Chris closed his eyes in utter relief and leaned in to kiss her, pulling her close to him.

"And I'm staying right here," Naomi whispered when he finally lifted his mouth from hers.

"What about Houston?" he asked, dazed. "You're not going to give up the chance to be a head of surgery because of me. I don't want you to do that. Evan and I can come with you to Houston."

She shook her head. "The hospital in Athens has already made me an offer to be the Chief of General Surgery and I want to take it. Besides, I have no family left in the States now, with both my parents gone. Athens is my home now. I was only going to leave because I couldn't bear to see you around if you didn't want me."

"I want you, Naomi. I've never stopped wanting you." He kissed her again. "I never want you to leave me and I'm going to make it impossible for you to do so. Even if it means constantly wining and dining you at the beach house or on the yacht. I can't live without you, *zoi mou*."

She kissed him. "That's definitely a start. And I love you, Chris. But remind me again what *zoi mou* means? You said it to me on Spritos too. My Greek's still a little rusty—although it's coming back to me in leaps and bounds now I'm forced to speak it daily."

"It means my life. You *are* my life, Naomi. You will always be my life, my heart and my soul. I can't live without you, *zoi mou*, and when we were apart, I wasn't really living. I love you."

"I love you too."

And they kissed again under the bright Athens moon, sealing their fate and breaking any kind of curse that had held them back. Real or imagined.

EPILOGUE

One year later

LISA HELPED HER finish buttoning up her simple wedding dress and then knelt down to fasten her sandals. Naomi had learned her lesson; she wasn't taking any chances on the winding streets of Mythelios.

She was going to walk down to the docks with her bridal party, and from there her future father-in-law's sporty yacht would take her to Spritos, where at a small chapel carved into the side of the cliff she was going to meet Chris and marry him.

It was the perfect spot—the place where she'd fallen in love with him again—and she wanted to make sure that it was going to go off without a hitch.

After he'd proposed, she would have married him the next day, but she hadn't wanted to take away from Lisa and Themo's wedding—or Deakin and Lea's, which had followed shortly after her cousin's. And then she'd had a lot of new responsibilities at one of Athens's largest city hospitals.

So, much to Chris's chagrin, they'd had a longer engagement than he'd wanted—but it would be worth it.

Or at least that was what she'd kept telling herself.

And then she'd found out she was pregnant, about

three months ago, and Chris had finally had enough of waiting. He'd quickly gone about getting a license so that they could finally get married.

He was so happy that she was pregnant, and that in a few months' time Evan was going to have a little brother or sister. She'd had to cut back on her responsibilities at the hospital, but she didn't mind. She didn't want to lose this child, and at her last checkup everything had been going well.

Her baby would have many little playmates. There was Theo and Cailey's little girl, as well as Lisa and Themo's baby, who had been born a few months after their marriage. Ares and Eri had tiny twin girls too, and Deakin and Lea were expecting their first child.

Evangelos was the eldest, and all those babies would have him to look up to. Evan was nearly two years old now, and Naomi loved him dearly. She and Chris had tried to reach out to his birth mother, to allow her to be in his life if she wanted to, but she'd turned them down.

Hopefully one day Lillian would want to see him, and not estrange herself from him the way that Chris's mother had done.

At least Nikos Moustakas had wised up. Even though Chris and his father still had things to work out between them, they'd had an excellent start and were well on the way to a better relationship.

And the clinic was thriving too, as Mythelios was finally rebuilt after the earthquake that had devastated the island over a year ago.

Everything was falling into place, and Naomi couldn't believe how happy she was. It was like a dream—although if it were, it was definitely one she didn't want to wake from.

"Do you think I'm dreaming?" Naomi teased.

Lisa laughed as she stood up. "When you have that baby, you'll soon realize this is no dream."

"I'm just so happy. I can't remember being this happy before in my life."

Lisa smiled at her and kissed her on the cheek. "I'm so happy that you're happy. If anyone deserves it, it's you, sweetheart. I'm so glad you decided to stay here. I should have said it last year, but with my wedding and you working in the hospital at all ungodly hours I forgot to tell you. I'm so glad that you're living here and that you're in my life. You're one of my best friends."

Naomi hugged her cousin. "I love you too."

"Now, let's get you down to that yacht and get you married."

"Thank you for being *paránymfos*."

Lisa beamed. "Of course. Who else would do it?"

They made their way down the steps of Chris's house. Chris and his *koumpáros* would already be at the church on Spritos.

As Naomi walked through the old town toward the docks, people called out their good wishes and gave her flowers—a small tradition that the people of Mythelios always bestowed upon a bride as she passed through the old part of the island on her way to town. Naomi was humbled, and by the time she got to the docks, she had quite the bundle of flowers in her hands.

Her *theíos* was waiting for her and Captain Panos helped her onto the yacht, getting her settled. Lisa took the posies of flowers and bound them with white ribbon. The rings and the *stefana* were at the church and had been blessed by the priest already.

Naomi was shaking. She was nervous. Not because she was uncertain, but because she couldn't wait to be married to Chris and start their life together. Finally.

It was only a short boat ride to Spritos.

At the bottom of a winding path one of her male cousins waited and helped her down, and then Lisa. Her uncle took her hand and Lisa led them up the path to the top of the cliff. Naomi's heart was beating extra-fast and she took a deep calming breath as the music started.

Lisa gave her a smile and then walked in ahead of her.

Her uncle gave her a kiss on her hand. "Your father would be proud of you. I'm sure that he is with us—and your mother."

Tears filled her eyes. "I'm sure they are too. Just as long as *Yia-yia* isn't!"

Her uncle laughed and squeezed her hand.

She took a deep breath and walked down the aisle toward her future.

Chris stood at the end, his *koumpáros*, Ares, standing beside him looking ridiculously handsome and boyish, with his long locks swept back and neat for once. Ares was grinning and clapping Chris on the shoulder, but Chris ignored him, his gaze locked on her.

As she walked up the aisle, she saw many familiar faces. There was Themo, holding his and Lisa's little girl. And there was Stavros and his wife, Maria, beaming.

Stavros had pulled through, and although his recovery had taken longer, due to his postoperative stroke, he was finally back to himself and was running the *taverna* with an iron fist like always.

Beside Stavros was Maximos and his mother. Maximos bowed his head in thanks for helping him. As did Giorgos and *his* mother.

Everyone who had touched their lives or had a hand

in bringing them together was here. Including Nikos Moustakas, who stood at the front holding Evangelos.

The little boy beamed and called out to her as she approached. All she could do was smile and wave to the boy she loved so completely. Evan didn't understand that he was supposed to be quiet.

Nikos lovingly hushed the toddler and smiled at her. He was a completely changed man. He was softer and kinder.

Her uncle lifted her veil and kissed her, and then took Chris's hand and placed it in hers. He put his hand over the top of Chris's, and in turn Chris kissed the top of her uncle's hand as a sign of respect.

Her uncle stepped back as the priest stepped forward and began chanting.

The *stefana*—two crowns of orange blossom connected with a ribbon—was passed over their heads three times to bless them, before being placed on their heads. And then the rings were brought forward.

Ares passed the rings back and forth over them three times, again to bless them, before handing the rings to Chris. Chris placed his ring on her finger and Naomi placed her ring on Chris's, not letting go her grip on him.

Then the chanting changed and Ares stepped behind them, taking the ribbon while Lisa lifted Naomi's train, and they all stepped forward in sync with the priest, walking around the altar.

Their eyes locked as they took their first steps together as man and wife.

They were married.

Once they'd returned to their spots, Lisa stepped back and Ares bowed and stepped back into his place.

The priest motioned to Chris and he leaned forward,

his hand still holding hers as they kissed. There were cheers and then he led her back down the aisle, holding her hand as they left the church and took the path down to the docks.

Nikos Moustakas's largest yacht, *The Epitome*, was waiting there, as that was where the reception was going to be.

"I wish we didn't have to have a big party and we could just sneak away to the beach house again. Or to our private cove," she said.

"I agree—but the reception is a big deal. There's a lot to celebrate, Dr. Moustakas." And he reached down to touch her belly, where their baby was growing.

She laughed. "I'm keeping Hudson for my professional life. I don't think I'll ever answer to anything else."

Chris laughed. "Whatever you say, *zoi mou*. I'm just glad you're mine and I'm never giving you up."

"Promise?" she asked.

"Promise."

And he kissed her again.

He would never stop kissing her for as long as he breathed.

* * * * *

LET'S TALK
Romance

For exclusive extracts, competitions
and special offers, find us online:

f facebook.com/millsandboon

◎ @millsandboonuk

𝕪 @millsandboon

Or get in touch on 0844 844 1351*

For all the latest titles coming soon,
visit millsandboon.co.uk/nextmonth

Want even more
ROMANCE?

Join our bookclub today!

'Mills & Boon books, the perfect way to escape for an hour or so.'

Miss W. Dyer

'Excellent service, promptly delivered and very good subscription choices.'

Miss A. Pearson

'You get fantastic special offers and the chance to get books before they hit the shops'

Mrs V. Hall

Visit millsandbook.co.uk/Bookclub and save on brand new books.

MILLS & BOON